MW00620221

BENEATH THE DUST

by

D.B. Barratt

Though many left the Midwest during the drought of the 1930's, others stayed, struggled and lived beneath the layers of dust and amid the depression of the times. This is the story of two such people, Johnnie Belle Veazey and Ralph Abraham Showalter.

Copyright © 2007 by D.B. Barratt

All rights reserved. No part of this book shall be reproduced or transmitted in any form or by any means, electronic, mechanical, magnetic, photographic including photocopying, recording or by any information storage and retrieval system, without prior written permission of the publisher. No patent liability is assumed with respect to the use of the information contained herein. Although every precaution has been taken in the preparation of this book, the publisher and author assume no responsibility for errors or omissions. Neither is any liability assumed for damages resulting from the use of the information contained herein.

This is a work of fiction. Names, characters, places, and incidents either are the product of the author's imagination or are used fictitiously. Any resemblance to actual events or locales or persons, living or dead, is entirely coincidental.

ISBN 0-7414-3894-0

Published by:

INFINITY
PUBLISHING.COM

1094 New DeHaven Street, Suite 100
West Conshohocken, PA 19428-2713
Info@buybooksontheweb.com
www.buybooksontheweb.com
Toll-free (877) BUY BOOK
Local Phone (610) 941-9999
Fax (610) 941-9959

Printed in the United States of America

Printed on Recycled Paper

Published May 2007

Acknowledgments

This novel was a work completed with the cooperation of my family as I interviewed, taped conversations, prodded memories and became emotionally involved, as intimate tales of a time gone by were voiced.

I want to thank my husband, Calvin Barratt, who believed in my success, gave encouragement and support for the many years of work, my children, Beth, Carrie, and John, who have each, in their own way, inspired me to go where my heart leads me, and my grandchildren, Trenton and Cody, who remind me that energy and joy come from following your passions.

The biggest thanks of all, however, must be given to my sisters and brothers, Nadine Hendrix, Ralph W. Showalter, Darlene LaBorde, Mary Howes, Betty Langosch, Beverly Beeney, Lynn Showalter, Kirk Showalter, Peggy Snyder, Connie Renne, Terry Showalter, Deborah Showalter-Johnson, and Cindy Showalter, who shared their lives, their time, and their thoughts about life "Beneath the Dust."

A special applause to my editor and mentor, Deborah Showalter-Johnson, who refused to let me be anything less than professional, and to my traveling companions during research about Star City, Arkansas, where we met and interviewed many wonderful people, I thank my sister, Connie Renne and my wonderful husband Calvin Barratt.

Prologue

Years after the death of Ralph Abraham, Johnnie Belle began to relate stories about her life in the 1930's when she left Star City, Arkansas, and rode a migrant truck north to Iowa with her brother to find work. It wasn't how she had envisioned her life to be. Though Star City didn't offer much, it was her life. Pushed from the nest, so to speak, Johnnie Belle moved as life flowed. She didn't know any other way. Johnnie Belle was never forced into making choices about life because her life was simple and she liked it that way. But that ended when she was 17. Between the effects of the national economy and nature's furious drought, her simple life became complex. The river of her life carried her out of Star City, Arkansas, and into northwest Missouri.

Ralph Abraham Showalter, father of seven children and widowed at the age of 33, was handsome, muscled, and hard-working. Since the death of his wife, he had focused on raising their children, working hard to put food on the table, and thinking about the future. He was a farmer with a businessman's head. He knew how to work the land and improve it, sell it and purchase another piece. He had no time to court a woman, and rarely socialized except for church on Sundays. Ralph faced challenges daily and it absorbed him emotionally. And, even with the physical labor required by the land, the mental challenges of doing business, and the joy of his children all gave him purpose; he could not seem to get over his loss and the loneliness it brought to him.

Two individuals facing a changing world, beneath the dust and depression, each alone as the journey begins...

Chapter 1

I never gave life a whole lot of thought. Star City, Arkansas was a small world to grow up in and it was all I knew. Cotton fields, putting up food from the garden, and helping Mama with the washing and ironing was what my life was all about. Nobody ever asked me what I wanted to be when I grew up. Girls like me were lucky to even make it through school because of having to work in the fields. Daddy died when I was too young to even know him and we were dirt poor. I had always stayed pretty close to Mama, but in the last few years things had changed. Mama got married again. Sister got married and moved off. Even Jack, my older brother had his eye on a special girl.

Time, didn't seem to stand still any more. It was beginning to wash across me like rapids come down from the mountains. I was carried along in the flow, not really aware of where I was headed or even really caring. Living in Star City was my life. I certainly was not interested in boys like my friend May Patterson, who made getting married her whole point in just living another day. I thought of boys as irritating and sometimes just plain no-good. I spent my time working, helping around the house, and keeping Harold out of trouble. At twelve it seemed he could find a lot of that. Books had been my only glance into the world beyond the front door, and though I wondered about things, I never yearned for more than I had. I was content. But, my contentment had been disrupted. The drought seemed to be unending. The cotton that came up this year was hard and dry, not fit for pickin'. There was no way for me to earn any money in this town. And that's why I stood here, in the dust and heat. I looked back toward town. I was doing what I never thought I would do in my whole life. I was saying good-bye to Star City and Mama at the same time.

I was scared, even with Jack right there beside me. He was four years older than my seventeen, and had always been protective of us "young-uns" as Mama called my sister, brother and me. Right now those four years didn't count for much as I looked at all those men sitting so close together on the board benches that had been hammered into the back of the old truck.

Letting Jack boost me into the open frame of the truck bed, I searched for an empty place to sit. I was filled with the terror of an unknown world, uncertainty about what we were doing, and the men around me.

It didn't help that I was small for my age. Mama said I looked a lot like her when she was sixteen, but I could not imagine Mama ever being sixteen, let alone having a small waist that called attention to a developing bosom. I folded my arms across my chest and held my bag close hoping to hide my body. Mama had cut my hair short, remade some of Harold's old britches for me and found an old worn hat that I pulled down nearly over my eyes to hide the best I could. I thought back over the months that Jack had talked about going up north. I never dreamed it would be like this. If I had it would have been a nightmare, not a dream.

I knew the way men would look at a woman some-times when one was "available" and it scared me. I had seen men look at Mama that way after Daddy died, though that didn't happen anymore since she'd married Mr. Jim.

Trying to hold back tears, I was feeling unsure and mixed up all of a sudden about this whole thing. I scrunched closer to Jack as men filled the back of the truck with their tote sacks full of the few possessions they'd need; their bedrolls tied up with rope.

Mama looked tearful herself as she handed Jack the sack with our food then moved back out of the way of the loading up. It had sounded so exciting when Jack had talked about us traveling to do field work and making our own money. Then he had seen the notices that they were hiring field hands for harvest up north. The drought that was going on over three years now had hurt all the cotton farmers around Pine Bluff and Star City.

There wasn't enough work to go around. Mama said the whole country was in a depression. President Roosevelt's plan was going to help once it got fully underway, but it didn't appear to be working fast enough for me. I wondered if President Roosevelt's plan included rain. In spite of myself I almost smiled.

Watching the others position themselves in the truck, I tried to remember all of the reasons Jack had used to get me to go with him, and how I felt a few days ago about what he called "the adventure of a lifetime." Why didn't Mama tell me to get down off that truck and get on back home? I looked hopefully past Jack and saw Mama standing on the road, my heart aching about as much as my stomach.

Though the sun was barely up, Mama already looked worn out standing there waiting to wave us on and I noticed how her old dress hung off her shoulder under the apron she always wore. That was the first time I ever looked at Mama from a distance and gave her any thought. Like the old pot on the cook stove, she was just always there, steady and unwavering, giving up her own existence to create a life for us. I didn't want to leave Mama now or ever, but I knew I was expected to make my own way and at least I had Jack.

Life had been hard on all of us, but especially Mama. Mr. Jim (we called him that since Mama began seeing him) didn't come to see us off. He was probably still sleeping off the state he'd got himself in the night before. Maybe it was his way of dealing with everything. Mama never said much. She just worked hard washing clothes for all the town folks. We never had much but Mama made sure our clothes were clean, we had food to eat, and when the cotton got picked we went to school. A lot of the poor kids didn't go to school and most of the girls never went more than the sixth grade. It didn't seem to make any difference in Star City as long as you could read.

I did not like school. It was bad enough we were poor, but Sister had a hearing problem and got teased all the time. Most of the kids thought she was just stupid. I hated the teachers for not helping her more and for their lack of understanding. But I did like to read. I wished I could have gotten hold of more books. What I'd read about I didn't always understand, but it did seem that if you searched hard enough, there were secret worlds hiding behind the words, waiting to be discovered.

I looked at Jack's face as he got down in front of me to cram the food sack under our bench with his clothes. How could he be grinning? Mama called me "mousy" because I never talked much and was always scared of people I did not know. But not Jack! He sat back down beside me and began waving at Mama and some friends like we were in a big parade! I would never understand the way he thought about life. I looked at Mama moving further back from the truck as others crowded forward to say their goodbyes. I waved too, and forced a smile, but I knew Mama could see the tears welling up in my eyes.

I watched her as the dry hot wind spit pellets of dirt up against her legs. Her brown hair was thin and pulled back into a ball. Wisps were flying over her ears and across her face and I noticed it was turning gray and wondered how long it had been like that. She had her arms crossed over her belly, leaning into her swayback, her broad feet spread out in the same old shoes she'd worn ever since I could remember. Swallowing hard, my throat choked back the sobs that were trying to erupt. There was more feeling swelling up in me at that moment than I had ever felt in my entire life. Anger, sorrow, fear and excitement was an explosive mix.

We didn't talk much, Mama and me, but we did have

an understanding and a closeness about things. I remembered the time she made me new bloomers from the old cloth flour sack and the big rose had ended right up on my backside. The wind blew my dress up at school and some kids hooted at me until I cried. Mama didn't make me wear them again and somehow they disappeared. Staring out through the haze, my memories flowed. I thought about the doll I got for Christmas when I was eight. Sister and I didn't often get dolls and we took real good care of the ones we had. I named mine "Ruby" since that was Sister's name, though we never called her that. Ruby, though scarred from frequent mending, was home sitting on my bed.

Every year for Christmas there was a new dress for my doll and candy for me. Our lives were simple, but happy. My heart ached for home and we hadn't even pulled out of town yet. It was going to be a long trip.

I watched as women waved to their husbands and sons. There was only one other girl on the truck. I knew she was Cody Jenkins' new wife from Pine Bluff, but I didn't know her name. I saw her look at me and I tried to smile. I hoped she was nice.

I heard the truck roar to a start and saw the smoke from underneath send people scrambling back away from the rear end. Two men grabbed a gate and pulled it down. I leaned back against the hard wooden side of the truck bed that was made to hold animals carted to market or maybe to hold boxes of peaches from spilling out as they were trucked out of Arkansas. The truck lurched and I watched as Mama half turned to walk back down the road towards home, her dress blowing in the breeze, a patch of dampness growing under her arm raised in one last wave of love. The heat from the sun was already sucking the sweat right out of everybody as the wind whisked across the dirt streets and sent grit into every crevice it could find.

"Mama," I mouthed silently.

All of a sudden my stomach lurched into my throat and I jumped to my feet, not caring about being looked at or about how much dirt I ate.

"Bye Mama." I yelled. "We'll write!"

I saw her stop and turn back around, slowly pulling the shoulder of her dress back up as she waved one last time.

I backed into my seat, unable to take my eyes off Mama and nearly landed in Jack's lap as the truck jerked again, grinding through the gears and dodging the ruts in the road.

I closed my eyes and lay my head across my own bed-roll. I thought about the day ahead for Mama. It was the same every day. Get breakfast for Harold and Mr. Jim, then head to the first house to do the washing. Mr. Jim might pick up an odd job or two to help with money to pay for his old truck and Harold would be left to tend the garden, anyway what was left of it. The drought had left most people with nothing but hard ground and dried up plants. We had carried some water from the well but just enough to save a few beans and turnips.

"Welp." Jack said still smiling and looking expectant like he was going to his wedding. "We are on our way now!"

I looked over at him. His expression dropped when he saw my face.

"You aren't going to change your mind now are you Johnnie Belle ? Why, you know yourself, there's nothing for you in Star City." He wiped his forehead with the back of his hand. "The whole world's out there just waiting for us to make our own way. Us, Johnnie Belle, you and me." He turned and looked at me, willing me to understand what was in his own heart. "Just think about it!"

"I know." I said bleakly. "But I miss Mama already."

I didn't say it very loud, but Jack heard me. I hugged my bedroll that I'd been gripping tightly and sighed. I wanted to know things about the world, but I didn't even know what questions to ask. Right now I felt tired and confused. I prayed that Jack really knew what we were doing and how this would all work out. I began to wonder why I had ever trusted him. He was always a big talker and pretended to know more than he really did, but I also knew that Jack had a way with people, and, he was my brother.

I saw Cody Jenkins put his arm around his wife and noticed the men on the truck began to shake hands and introduce themselves to each other. Most of them were smiling and talking and acting pretty happy. I knew their spirits were up because work would give them money to send home to their families. I was glad for them because I knew what struggles families faced these days.

"Jack, how long will it be? I mean 'til we get to Iowa?"

"I figure," Jack rubbed his chin, "About two or three days if it doesn't rain any and there's not much chance of that."

The man sitting across from us was straddling the old board bench that ran down the center of the truck. He must have heard us talking because he looked over at Jack, took his hat off and said, "Dependin' more on how this old truck runs."

Jack stuck out his hand and the man did the same. "Name's George Camp, from east of Pine Bluff. Glad to meet ya'."

"Jack Veazey. And my sister, Johnnie Belle."

I looked at the man from the tops of my eyes as I pulled my old rolled up quilt further up in front of my face. I was as shy as Jack was forward. Can't figure the Good Maker molding a brother and a sister to be so different.

"Ma'am." The man nodded at me. I nodded back at him but kept my bedroll pulled close and my head down.

Jack opened the sack of food Mama sent and handed me some bread. I took it, but not because I was hungry. I still hadn't found my tongue yet and I felt nervous. Harold would call me an old fraidy-cat.

As the truck rumbled, I closed my eyes to the soft noise of conversation between the men around me, and I began to wonder when we would get to the first town. There were still a few places left on the truck to sit and I figured we'd stop and pick up others. Jack and I had seen crop teams head north before. Some of the men came back and some didn't. Last year Tate Edwards went and when he got back to Star City he had enough money to buy his own place and ask Pearly Mason to marry him. I guess that's what did it for Jack. Mary Jacobs had her eye on Jack and he figured he could make as good as Tate did. This summer Mary had gone down to Hope to be with her sister who was having a baby. Jack might not have been so happy about leaving Star City either if Mary Jacobs had been standing in that road along with Mama.

Mama had made it clear that she would not let me be a wash woman like her. She wanted me to go along with Jack, save up my money and move to the city. I didn't know what I'd do in a city, but I wanted to please Mama, and Jack was always pushing me to "spread my wings." Mr. Jim didn't seem to care one way or the other. Since Sister got married last year and moved off and Harold was near old enough to pull his own weight in the cotton fields, here I was, jumping right out of my nest and wondering where in the heck I would fall!

My body flew forward, then back again against Jack and I realized I had fallen asleep and the truck had stopped.

"Where are we?" I asked Jack, stretching across the tight space where I sat.

"Oh, somewhere near the Missouri border, I reckon." Jack stood up to stretch as he waited for two men to pull up the truck gate that held us in. Most of the men were talking and laughing, like they were all old friends getting together. Yet I noticed they each grabbed their bags to carry off the truck as though they didn't trust anyone. I stood up to take my turn getting off the back end of the truck with Jack right in front of me. Between the slats of the truck sides, I saw a few houses and a small park. As I got to the edge of the truck, Cody Jenkins' wife was there and she smiled at me. Jack turned around and held out his arms as if to help me.

I jumped off and dropped my bag spilling some of my clothes on the ground and quickly crouched down to shove them all back in. Cody Jenkins wife was taller than me and she jumped down right next to my mess.

"Here," she said as she helped me to stuff my things back into the burlap.

"Thanks," I said feeling glad to have her there to help me. "I guess my legs are kind of stiff from riding so long."I looked around blinking at the dust swirls that rose from the road around us like clouds before a storm.

"This here's Millfield." some man announced. "Water over there and outhouses that-a-way. We'll be taking off again in one hour."

We all looked in the direction he had pointed, then back at each other. I was trying to tie the string around my sack tighter.

"My name's Cindy Jenkins." Cody's wife had a low voice that reminded me of a teacher I had back in school. She watched me tie up my stuff as Cody came around from the side of the truck.

"Cindy," Cody's face shone when he looked at her, "Let's go up on that rise and eat some lunch with Jack and Johnnie Belle. You guys meet each other?" Cody put his hand in Cindy's and looked at me.

She nodded, smiled and turned to walk up the hill with

Cody.

"Come on!" Cindy yelled back over her shoulder as they began to run.

"Sounds good to me." Jack said and followed, loping across the barren park, his own expression of joy at being freed from the confines of our journey. Carrying the sack of food and his own tote sack of clothes, he reminded me of pictures I had seen of Santa Claus and I had to smile. I took a big gulp of the dry hot air and felt happy just to stand up.

I followed them, glad to walk and inhale air that didn't smell like truck fumes. At the top of the slope Cindy was spreading out a blanket.

"Put your tote-sack down and let's go to the outhouse, Johnnie Belle." Cindy said softly.

"All-right." I said, a little embarrassed but glad all the same.

As we left the boys behind, Cindy kicked at the dust making clouds and said, "You don't talk much do you?"

"No. I guess I don't." I kept my eyes on the outhouse and wondered if it would have one hole or two. I wasn't one to share an outhouse either.

"You go first." Cindy looked at me kindly. "I'll watch the door."

I knew then that I would like her. Somehow she understood my shyness.

"Thanks." I went in and took my turn and I heard Cindy humming. It reminded me of Mama. Mama would always hum or sing or whistle around the house. When I was finished, I waited for her. The wind was hot as it moved up the rise and it brought lots of the dirt from the road that stuck to the sweat on my skin.

"Let's go." Cindy said as she came out of the old

wooden shed still buttoning up the front of the old pants she was wearing. She looked as strange in those pants as I felt in mine. We walked easily together.

"How old are you?" She asked me lazily.

"I'm 17 and a half." I told her and then wished I hadn't added the half because it sounded like something a child would say.

"I'm only 18,"she said. "But I'll be 19 before Christmas."

"Me too. I mean my birthday is just a few days before Christmas." I was surprised at myself for speaking up. "When's yours?"

"December first. How about yours?"

"The 23rd." I replied and we began to run lightly down the hill. I wasn't sure if it was the break from the ride, or just the feeling that I had made a new friend, but I felt happy all the same.

Cindy's long yellow hair was up in a pony tail and she too wore a man's shirt that was bigger than need be. She was about the same height as Sister but slimmer built. I noticed she had polish on her nails, but she didn't wear make-up. She was pretty in a country sort of way. Not like one of those girls I'd seen on the front of the magazines in Byer's Grocery back home, but natural and healthy looking all the same. I wished I was taller. At least my hair was a good color of brown and not that white stuff I was born with. Mama still called me towhead.

"Are you going all the way to Iowa or just to Missouri?" I had begun to feel less nervous and was interested to know if I could count on her company for awhile longer on the trip.

"Cody says we're going wherever the work pays the most and settle down. I'm kind of excited and kind of scared.

He's done this before and says if you work around you can find a place to sharecrop and make some money to put toward a place of your own. I want to have a baby soon as we can afford it."

I looked up at her and she must have seen the shock on my face.

"My sisters are all married," she went on, "and they have babies. I helped them back home and I just love babies."

"My sister got married last year." I told her. "But she doesn't have any babies yet."

Personally I hoped Sister didn't have babies for a long time because I had the feeling that Bobby would not be a good daddy to any baby.

The boys had opened up the food and were already sharing it between them.

"Here, Johnnie Belle," Jack said as he handed me a piece of cold chicken.

"So you think you're going to stop in Iowa or keep going further north, Jack?" Cody Jenkins asked as Cindy and I both settled down on the blanket and began to eat.

"I'm one to play it by ear." Jack said, his mouth full of cornbread.

"A couple of the men told us that there isn't much work in the Dakota's and even Nebraska is still trying to get their fields back to where they can grow crops again, but could be they just don't want competition from us younger fellows." He grinned at Cindy.

"Somebody said Missouri had plenty of beans to pick, and some corn, but the wheat just dried up again." Jack added. He paused as if reflecting on his own words then leaned down resting his body on his elbow and looked at the sky. "They say the sky stayed black for three days in a row last month in Oklahoma."

I chewed slowly and drank the lemonade which was no longer cold and was watery from the melted ice Mama had spared us. We were all quiet, thinking about that dust and drought and the distress we knew the whole country was in.

"What'll we do, Jack, if there's no work?" I spoke softly looking at Jack, going over the conversation he and Cody had been having.

"Oh, there's work up there all right." Jack didn't look worried, so I figured he and Cody had just been talking like men like to do when they want to appear like they know something. I'd heard Mr. Jim and his friends sitting under the shade tree in front of our house sorting through the possibilities of life, yet coming up with no real answers. I could never really understand that kind of talk. I did not see the point of idle conversation. If something was worthy of talk then I surely hoped it would result in some conclusion or direction.

One thing about being quiet was that I learned a lot by listening. Mama always told us stories about how she'd hear the men sitting around talking about the world and the way things were, but never getting up and doing anything to make any difference. In school it was always the girls gossiping on about nothing, so I guess maybe they got most of it out of their systems by the time they grew up and the menfolk took to doing it. Finishing the food, I felt full and the breeze was nice even if it did stir up the dust.

Cindy lay down with her head across Cody's chest and he put his hand on her waist. I watched them relax together and thought that it must be nice to have a man to share your life with, someone who really cared about you in a special way. I could see that Cody did care about Cindy. Yes, Cindy was a lucky girl.

Jack jumped up. "Come on, Johnnie Belle. Let's go for a walk."

I got up cramming our stuff back into the bag.

"Aw, leave it for now." Jack said. "We'll be back."

"Ok." I dropped all the stuff and caught up with Jack as he took off in that long lean stride of his. He was not a very patient fellow.

"I suppose they just might like a moment to themselves." Jack smiled at me.

I turned red in the face and looked at him. "Oh." It was all I could manage, realizing that I had been staring at them earlier.

I was glad Jack thought about things like that. I just had never met a boy that made me have feelings like those between Cody and Cindy.

I asked Jack, "Do you think I'll ever really grow up?"

"Sure, you will, Johnnie. Just don't be in any hurry. And don't worry about it. It'll happen when it happens."

I wasn't sure if Jack meant my body would change or I'd meet some man, but I wasn't about to ask him. I hardly even talked to Sister about that. I knew Mama knew that I thought about those things because she always had the right words to say at the right time without me explaining. But we never talked out-right about personal things.

When I was packing for the trip, Mama brought in a sack and handed it to me. I took the sack and looked at her. Neither one of us said anything but I knew what she was giving me just by the look in her eyes. I just stuck it in the bottom, below all my clothes embarrassed about that God-given part of what a woman is all about. Life was a mystery and that was a fact.

Jack and I had passed the truck and headed toward town. There were three buildings that held each other up on one side of the street and two that seemed able to stand alone on the other side. The building in the center of the three had a barber's pole, though it was dirty enough you had to look close to be sure. There was a bench there and two men sat reading an old paper. Two trucks were parked near the edge of the dirt street, and an old dog lay in the shade beneath the trucks drumming his tail and stirring up more dust. Other than that the place looked to be a ghost town. Guess it was too hot and gritty to be outside unless you had to be. Next to the barber was a small grocery and we went in. Jack bought a root beer for us to share and the man behind the counter asked if we were traveler's from the truck he'd seen come into town.

Jack told him we were, and he talked to Jack about where we were headed. I listened. The man said we were the third truck that had stopped this week.

"You two look like brother an' sister." He drawled as he put his foot up on the counter.

It was our eyes, I thought. Mama always said we had the same hazel eyes.

"We are." Jack stuck out his hand. "Name's Jack Veazey and this here's my sister, Johnnie Belle. We're from Star City and heading up north."

The man nodded my way and I looked down at my feet. I wondered how I got such big feet when I wasn't very big anywhere else.

"Things are bad ain't they?" He asked but didn't seem to be expecting any answer. "Why, they say the dust is higher than any snow they ever seen out Oklahoma ways."

"Dryer than Mama's laundry after three days on the line in July." Jack looked at me and winked. He was always coming up with some stupid way to say what he was thinking and he knew what I thought about it. Mary Jacobs called it "wit". A nit-wit is what I thought.

Jack was a thinker and he liked words. In that way we were some alike, I guess. He handed me the bottle of root beer and I finished it off and put it in the box that was there on the floor next to the ice box. The heat was building so I went to stand in the door way to get some of the moving air being pulled in by a fan on the ceiling.

"I seen a lot of youngsters heading north and west in the last few years. I guess there's nothing to keep 'em down here since the drought and then the hoppers. Ain't seen nothin' like it afore." He spit into a can that was beneath the old wooden counter.

"Here." He grabbed a newspaper and held it out for me. "You read?"

"Yes sir." I replied looking at the paper.

"Then take it and read it. I'm through with it. Hate to waste all them words."

You'd think he had been reading my mind. I walked over glad to have it. Back home we never could afford to buy a paper but I did sometimes get to read an old one that Mama brought home from one of her washing jobs.

"Thank you." I said finally looking up at him. I folded the paper and put it under my sticky arm and went to stand by the door again.

"Well," Jack drawled as slowly as the man behind the counter. I figured he'd probably spit too if he knew how. "Guess we'd better be heading back, Johnnie Belle."

I reached to open the screen door just as Jack grabbed it and held it for me. I knew he was just showing off, trying to look older than he was. But I didn't mind. Jack was alright.

Jack and I headed back toward the park. There seemed to be no end to the blowing dirt and stifling heat. Sweat was trickling down my back. We walked slowly, looking toward the truck where the driver had put the hood up and looked to be filling it with water.

"I'm going up to the outhouse." I said. "I'll meet you in a few minutes."

"See you." Jack waved and he trotted up the hill towards where we had left Cody and Cindy.

I headed up the rise and knocked at the door of the old wooden structure that had "women" written on it once upon a time. You could still make it out but it wouldn't be long before it was completely gone. No one answered so I slowly opened the door and peeked in. The smell wasn't too bad, but I still tried to hold my breath. It was something I had done since I was little and it was just habit. I guess I didn't want any of the smell from any privy inside my head. When I had finished and come out the door, I was about ready to pass out. I ran towards the blanket before I gasped for breath. Jack was there sitting on the grass and then I saw Cody and Cindy up by the well refilling their jars with water.

"Guess we'd better do that too." I said as I bent over to grab my jar. Jack grabbed his and we headed in that direction. We met Cody and Cindy.

Then we heard a man yell that it was time to load up.

The four of us looked down at the truck and saw the men all ambling that way.

"We'll fold the blanket and wait for you guys." Cindy said as she and Cody headed back up the hill.

Jack and I took our turns at the well, then returned to grab our tote sacks and walked back to the truck with Cody and Cindy.

We joined the line to get back onto the rickety truck . Jack helped me climb in and I shoved my sack under my seat, held onto my bedroll and sat down watching the others do the same. Some of the men had taken different places so Cindy and Cody put their stuff under the boards beside Jack and me, then sat and leaned against the boards.

"Let's see here now." The man who was in charge was counting heads. "Looks like everybody's ready." He scratched his head and fanned himself with his hat. "We gonna run this truck up to near Springfield, Missouri and spend the night. There's a place to camp. After that we be head'in on north to I-o-weigh." He stretched it into three syllables which made it sound important. "We got a job waitin' for us there. They got a bunk house."

We all listened intently, anxious to know details about what our crew would be doing. I wondered how I'd feel about this trip after a few days in the field trying to keep up with all these men then heading back to a bunkhouse to sleep. Jack looked at me. I wondered if he was thinking the same thing. The man with the information put his hat back on and went to get in the cab of the truck. The motor roared, shaking everything and everybody, the exhaust spit out black smoke, and we started moving down the road.

As we went through town, I saw the two old men still sitting on the bench, reading, their shirts wet from sweat. The dog hadn't moved from his shade. Dust swirled through the ripples of heat waves that were almost unbearable. If it weren't for the speed of the moving truck stirring up the air, I think I would have lost all that food I ate back at the park.

"Springfield, Missouri." Jack said. "That's a fur piece. We're gonna be mighty sore of riding in this here truck by the time we get there."

Cody bent over, leaned his elbows on his knees, put his head on his hands and looked at me. "Well, Johnnie Belle," he questioned. "What do you think about all this?"

I smiled and shook my head. "I guess it can't be any worse than back home." I thought about that for a minute and went on. "Or then, maybe it could."

Cindy smiled at me and laughed a deep laugh, but not unlady-like. "Maybe we'll all settle the same place." She said eagerly, probably hoping I'd be there to help with that baby she was wanting to have.

"Not me." said Jack. "I got plans to earn money and

go back. Hope to get married."

"Jack!" Cody beamed, probably glad to see someone else on the verge of the life he was currently enjoying. "Which one of those sweet young things you got your eye on?"

"Mary Jacobs." Jack said her name gently. I knew he did indeed have feelings for her by the look on his face.

"Mary Jacobs?" Cindy almost squealed. "Why we go to the same church. She went to help her sister with the new baby this summer." She looked excited at this news. "Have you asked her yet?"

"Course I've asked her." Jack drawled. "She would of married me before we left but her sister needed her and I need to get some money together to get us a place to settle down. She won't hear of leaving Star City with all her sisters there." Jack smiled.

"Congratulations." Cody held out his hand and Jack shook it. Some of the men were looking over and smiling. We were going to be a close group. Like it or not.

"Now all we've got to do is find Johnnie Belle a man." Cindy declared, her face lighting up.

"Never you mind about that." I leaned back against the old truck to close my eyes and think about Mama.

Chapter 2

He let the truck roll to a stop in front of the old church that held memories from his childhood. Feeling empty of energy, he sat there watching the dust from the road hover in the air as if waiting patiently to find a place to settle. Gazing at the worn structure, the steeple's peeling boards, he knew it should be painted before the summer was over. He'd talk to some of the other men about it when he had time.

Ralph usually moved with a steady purpose, but for the moment he appeared content to ramble, at least mentally. He picked up his old handkerchief from where he'd dropped it on the seat, wiped across his brow, and pushed his hat back off his forehead. It was a habit he was not really aware he had. Then he purposefully turned his head toward the graveyard.

For a few moments he just sat there staring, though not at all seeing the curved shape of the iron above the gate with the words Tharp's Grove Cemetery molded into place. Nor was he able to focus on that which was just inside the iron fence. His head was turned in the right direction and his eyes were open, but his mind was looking backward in time.

There in that private space somewhere deep inside of his head floated the only vision that penetrated his thoughts. There he saw Bessie. She was standing at their kitchen table holding a baby in her arms. Her soft auburn hair was pulled back but strands had come loose and they were tucked behind her ears. Flour was dusted across her face as she rocked her body back and forth, cradling the baby in a blanket and holding the bundle closely at her breast. It was a soft memory. Unsure why this particular memory was the one he seemed to hold on to while others faded, Ralph decided it was probably because he loved her way of mothering the children more than anything else about her.

Looking up, he was unaware of how much time had passed when the apparition left him, and he lowered his head slowly feeling the ache of his loss once again. Tears beaded in his eyes and for a moment the world spun out of control as he allowed the reality of life to seep back into his soul where emotion ruled. Bessie was not at home any more, nor would she ever hold their babies again. Bessie was forever locked inside that iron fence in a grave in the family plot. Pulling the lever on the door, he angrily pushed himself out of the truck letting the heavy metal swing wide as it succumbed to the gravity of the land.

Ralph Abraham Showalter pushed his hat back again and paused beside the truck bed as though unsure about what he was doing there. Then, not bothering to shut the door he moved somberly across the dry earth towards the iron fence. Gently shoving the gate aside and moving hesitantly past the fence, he walked to the patch of dried ground that held his wife. He stopped, his head bent downward, but his eyes still clutching to the vision in his mind. It had been nearly five years since they'd buried her there, yet it seemed like only yesterday that Ralph had been forced to move on alone.

He sighed and focused his eyes on the reality of her grave. Today, he needed her.

Standing there alone he thought he could hear her voice. It calmed him and he looked up and out, across the ragged state of the graveyard that spread over the sloping hillside, held prisoner by the heavy fencing.

More out of habit than an effort for neatness, Ralph squatted down and pulled at a few weeds. He looked up at the sky and swiped at the back of his neck. It had been some time since he had visited his wife's grave. He never had been one to come out here and talk to Bessie as though she were still alive. His way was to burrow into work and try to keep all their kids headed in the right direction. It was tough. Life married to Bessie had been good. She gave him seven children. And in the end that's what took her.

He had thought when the banks failed, that things were about as shaky as they could get. Life had changed a lot for most folks with money in short supply. Then Bessie died leaving him not only with a great loss to absorb but also with a week-old infant and six other children to raise, alone. Now after years of drought and trying to survive making a living trucking anything he could, there was a new struggle to deal with. Beverly, only eight, was sick and it was bad. His strength of body, mind and soul seemed to have drained away.

"Bessie," Ralph ventured. "We're not doing so good."

He coughed nervously and looked around as if someone might see him. "Nadine graduated from high school this past spring and little Lynn is growing like a weed. The other girls all help out when they aren't bickering back and forth. Ralph Wendell is pretty much off on his own. He paused and swallowed hard. Beverly's sick, Bessie."

Ralph choked up. He was a man who could think quickly on his feet and make smart decisions in a snap. Good with business dealings Ralph could do math in his head faster than the banker could figure up on paper. He liked to be in control, one step ahead, but this was one time the situation controlled him. Coping skills would have to take over as his ability to think and make things happen was not working.

"The doc said Beverly's got to get shots every day for a year or more or she'll die. The doc and me talked about it, Bessie."

Scratching his head, he picked at another weed. "He knows I drive two hours to get down there, then back. He knows that I have little Lynn to care for and that the girls are trying to get their education. That's where I've been all day, Bessie, at the hospital talking it all out with him and little Beverly. I'm worn, Bessie, just plum worn all out."

He sat down and put his head in his hands. The grass

was so dry it was poking at his legs through his pants, but he didn't notice. He glanced back down the road and over at the church then sighed. He looked up at the sky as though he felt his communication might be better directed upwards.

"Bessie, Doc said he'd take her. He said he'd take Beverly to live with him and his wife. They haven't been able to have children and they'd give Beverly a good home and be able to get her healthy."

Ralph paused and took a breath realizing that he had known there was no real decision to make. There was simply no choice here.

"There doesn't seem to be any other way, Bessie."

He looked at his rough hands calloused from work that never ended and studied his old work boots that needed replacing a long time ago.

"I know they'll do fine by her."

His voice was neither encouraging nor sad. It was simply stating fact. He shook his head and admitted as much to himself as to the one who lay silent and still. "I know that's what we'll have to do."

Looking back down at her grave, Ralph sensed Bessie's steady gaze and felt the load was shared. "I just needed to tell you about it Bessie. I just needed to talk it out with you. I wanted you to understand."

His mind lay blank, empty, unaware of thought or emotion. Unmoving he waited. Not for a sign, and not because he did not want to leave, but waited for life to fill him once again and acknowledge that it was time to pick up and go on. It was a familiar feeling he would recognize from those days right after Bessie took sick and the doctor told him she wouldn't make it.

Slowly, unconsciously, the growing emotions that connect the brain and the heart began to collide with thoughts of his children. Considering the decision he had made, he wondered how he would be able to tell the kids. His solitude there at her grave had given him bits of confidence at which he desperately began to grab. He could feel the control returning. He knew he would be able to go on, though slowly, one foot in front of the other, one day at a time. Doing what needed to be done, he would work, sleep and eat, gaining momentum as each day trickled by.

"When I tell the kids I need to feel firm about it." Ralph said aloud. "I do now, Bessie. I do now."

Ralph allowed himself to dwell for awhile on the kids and how it would be when he told them about Beverly. They had been through so much together. They'd probably take it better than he was. Saying it out loud, here, helped. He stood up and looked once more toward the heavens. His belief was powerful and he knew that God did not need for him to speak his feelings aloud or silently. He believed that God was capable of absorbing all that was welling up in his aging body and to understand him better than he understood himself. Like the old church hymn he'd learned in church as a boy, he knew he needed to "Trust and Obey."

After a moment, he looked down again.

"Well, Bessie, I've got to get on home." Ralph stared at the grave feeling once again the loss he had suffered, the pain he still had. His shoulders shook as a sob caught in his chest. He wanted to cry but he knew he wouldn't let himself, even here, with no one to witness it. He was a man and he didn't cry. Besides that he had to keep moving on. At least that's what he told himself.

Ralph walked slowly across the cemetery to the gate, pulled it to, and latched it shut. Then he walked over to the truck and slid into the seat. The sun was still fairly high up, but his stomach told him that it was nearly suppertime. Tired and depleted from a different kind of exertion than that of a normal day, he wearily reached for the door handle and pulled it with a strong arm to slam it back into place. Shoving his hat back, he turned the key that could always be found, left there in the ignition.

Life had taught Ralph that one often had to make a new path through the mire of whatever came along. He was not afraid of hard work, new ideas, or finding his own way. Independence had been instilled in him by his own father who had lost his own young wife when Ralph was a boy.

Letting out on the clutch, he rolled out of the church-yard onto the dirt path that some called a road. He headed the truck towards home. His mind had already arrived.

Darlene and Nadine would hopefully be getting supper on and probably arguing over whose turn it was to do the dishes tonight. Mary and Betty would be practicing the piano, and Aunt Emma and Uncle Loren would be along soon with Lynn.

As much as Ralph thought his older sister Emma was a spoiled brat, she had been helpful with the younger two. He favored the help from his older brother, Davy and his wife Ruth because they were more practical than Emma. Ruth helped the girls with household chores and taught them cooking and sewing skills. Emma would baby-sit but she also put too many ideas about new fangled things in the older girls' heads. Between them, Emma and Ruth did manage to be there for the girls in a way he was not able to do. He could not have made it through those first few years without his own family to help him.

The sun was in his eyes as he headed due west and the dust once again swirled about in his mirror as though teasing the sky with an assault. But the sky remained still and unthreatened. No bolt of lightening, bang of thunder or even mere cloud raised its head to stare the dry ground down, back to where it belonged. With no flicker of a fight, the charging dust passively draped itself down the edge of the road blanketing the puckers of hard yellow stubble to await the next free puff of wind that would probably not come until Sunday morning when people headed to church.

It didn't take more than fifteen minutes before his place came into view. The old oak that was taller than the house itself was one of the reasons they bought here. It provided shade in the summer and some protection from the cold winds of the winters. The kids could climb in it and the rope swing rarely lacked a companion. The outbuildings needed fixing up but one was good enough to keep a few chickens for eggs. Further across the valley he saw Smith, his neighbor, herding his cows in to milk. Ralph would never understand Emma preferring store milk and store bought ice cream. Maybe tonight they'd just have to get out the churn and make some good homemade stuff.

As he pulled up next to the house, the dust from the old farm road continued to escort him. Even as he climbed slowly out of the vehicle and walked towards the back porch, the swirl of thick dirt appeared to have a life of its own. Bessie had hammered big nails for him to hang his old work clothes on just inside the torn screen door. It occurred to him that he couldn't remember the last time he'd used the front door. Bessie had told him he was always too dirty to come through the house that way, especially since they'd laid the new linoleum. He remembered his mother telling him the same thing once. Ralph wondered how much his children would remember of their mother. His children needed a mother. He knew that, but he was too darn busy just getting from one day to the next to do anything about it. He pulled the screen door open and walked into the house.

As the door slammed behind him, he pulled off his old boots and hung up his hat. The beans smelled good and he hoped the girls had made more cornbread because he'd eaten the last of it that morning. When he had time to hunt, they had rabbit, squirrel and sometimes a possum or a coon to eat. Once in awhile, they'd butcher a chicken but most of the time they ate beans and cornbread. He bought the beans and cornmeal both by the sack full and the girls knew how to cook it. Ralph wasn't one to worry about what they ate as long as everybody got full. Variation in foods that got served was not a concern that ever entered his mind. Getting full was.

He saw the old pot on the cook stove full of warm beans and saw the cakes of cornbread stacked near it. They knew enough to cook the bread before the heat of the day and nobody minded eating it cold. Darlene was sitting at the table darning some socks and Nadine was standing at the stove stirring at the beans and probably trying to scrap the scorched part from the bottom of the pot.

"Supper ready?" He asked no one in particular.

"We're ready when you are." Nadine began to dish the beans into bowls.

"Darlene get the butter, will you?" Nadine took charge easily. Even before her mother died she was able to manage the place.

"Betty, Mary, can you help get the milk in the glasses?" Nadine yelled but not unkindly. "I see Uncle Loren and Aunt Emma pulling up now. Darlene see if they want to stay for supper."

"I'm going to see if Uncle Loren brought us candy." Betty scrambled out the front door knowing that Aunt Emma would never enter through the back with all of Dad's old dirty work clothes kept there.

Mary came in and got the pitcher of milk out of the icebox. "Dad how was Bev?"

"A mite better I'd say. She wanted to know what everybody here was doing. Did you girls clean up upstairs like I told you to?"

Ralph didn't much notice when things were a mess but he had gone up to get some of Beverly's clothes and he couldn't make heads or tails out of the girl's room.

Mary finished pouring milk and she set the cornbread from the stove onto the oak table, got a knife and cut it into individual portions.

"Well, Darlene said she didn't have enough room for her clothes in the dresser." Mary looked at her with a scowl.

Darlene decided to just keep quiet. What could she say since it was true. She knew that hoarding that drawer would one day come to an end and she was prepared.

"She's got one whole drawer full of her old paper dolls. She must have paper dresses enough for fifty dolls in there," Mary said disgusted.

"But we did get everything folded up in stacks."

"Is that right, Darlene?" Ralph questioned her but just for the record because he knew it was probably true. His girls argued and bickered but they did not lie.

"Yes." Darlene's mind was already picturing the next place she could keep her dress designs.

Ralph sighed. He never was sure of himself with the girls. Darlene had cut paper doll clothes for those paper dolls ever since he could remember. Guess she'd been stashing them all these years. He'd have to get her to throw them out because they didn't have room for another dresser and Mary was old enough now to share some of the drawer space.

"There's just four drawers Dad and I need two and Darlene has one with her clothes and the other with those dolls." Nadine walked to the table carefully balancing two bowls of beans at a time.

"It's time for her to grow up anyway." Successful at getting the soup to the table without spilling a drop, she put her hands on her hips the way she'd seen her Mother do and looked at Darlene.

"Why, she doesn't do anything around here when you leave, either."

Now Nadine's hands were in the air, another sign of her Mother's.

"She sews and reads and cuts out doll dresses all day long. But if I try to tell her to get to her chores she just sasses me."

Nadine noticed the tablecloth was a little dirty but it would get washed when it got washed. Anyway the bowls would cover up the spots. If the others would help out more she would be able to keep the house better.

She was to start business school in two months and she had enough to do without doing the washing more than once a week. That reminded her that she needed to talk to Dad about some new fabric for a dress and Aunt Emma said she needed to get a slip. Maybe Aunt Emma would bring it up for her because talking to Dad about private things had not been easy. He just didn't understand.

Before the conversation could go further they heard the front screen door screech open.

"Hello!" Uncle Loren called out coming through the front door, his huge frame contradicting his gentle manner. Aunt Emma was the exact opposite, small and fragile looking, but bossy.

"In here." Ralph called from the kitchen where he had sat down near the table ready to eat as soon as the girls got through tattling on each other.

"Going to join us for supper?"

"Oh thanks, Ralphie." Emma walked into the kitchen and kissed Ralph's cheek. "We just ate ice cream at the store and I couldn't eat another bite!"

Betty pushed herself between Aunt Emma and Uncle Loren and into the kitchen all the while sucking on a stick of sugar and gripping more in her other hand. She put the extras on the table for the others to share. Ralph didn't mind. It was one of the few store bought treats his kids had. Money was too hard to make to throw it away on candy, so when Emma and Loren gave it to the kids, he let them have it.

Loren and Emma owned the little grocery in town. Craig was a growing area. Uncle Loren owned the store and a gasoline pump and there was a Nazarene Church, a Methodist Church, and a park with a water tower that Ralph had climbed more than once when he was a boy. In fact, Loren and Emma's back yard bordered that very park and their little house was in the shadow of that very water tower.

Loren ambled behind Emma taking his hat off.

"Emma, we've got to get back to town. I need to finish putting out the new supply of notions that arrived today."

"What did you find out today, Ralphie?" She asked him with some subtlety not totally ignoring her husband but needing to find out.

Ralph paused, looked up at the couple then around at the girls who were pulling out chairs to sit down to eat. Lynn was just coming in through the back door.

"Daddy!" He yelled. "We're home! Did you see Bev today?"

Ralph grabbed him and gave him a little rough and tumble hug.

"Yes, I saw Beverly today. She said she missed you."

"Look at this bug I found." Lynn opened his chubby sun browned hand and Ralph saw a scrawny beetle there.

"Go throw him back outside and wash your hands. It's time to eat."

Lynn ran back out through the back porch, slammed the screen door and turned around doing the same coming back in.

"Don't slam that door, Lynn! I've told you that a hundred times." Nadine shook her finger towards the little boy thinking how glad she would be in two months to live in Chillicothe where the business school was. Dad had found her an older woman to stay with.

Lynn ignored her for the one hundred and first time and sat down at his place at the table.

Darlene got up and took Lynn by the hand. She didn't have to say anything as he allowed her to lead him over to the wash bowl and wash up. By now Lynn, whom some pitied because he had no mother, had learned to deal with his fate of having more mothers than most boys had bad dreams about.

Seeing Emma and Loren were waiting for an answer, and all the kids were there together, except for Ralph Wendell, who was rarely home anymore, Ralph decided he might as well get this settled once and for all. They were a family even though sometimes it didn't feel like it since Bessie died and it was important for them to face things together.

"Well, I was at the hospital today with Beverly, and the doctor said Beverly is doing better. But, that's because she is getting the shots she needs."

He looked around at the girls and knew they were quietly waiting to hear if they would lose Beverly now, too, like their Mother. They had faced too much at their age. He saw it especially in Nadine's eyes. She was older in many ways than her 16 years should have allowed for.

"I could bring her home but I'd have to take her back and forth to Saint Joseph to the hospital every day to get the shots she needs."

He was getting it out, but for the first time in a long time he found talking was not an easy task.

"Daddy, why's she got to get shots?" Lynn, only five, didn't miss a thing.

"Well, the doc explained it all but if she doesn't get the

medicine from the shots she will be really sick." Ralph was gentle but tired sounding.

"Could she die?" Mary asked, her eyes wide with fear.

"Well I suppose anyone could die." Ralph tried to avoid discussing that part of it.

"But the doctor said that he and his wife have a big house with extra bedrooms and they want to let Beverly stay with them until she is all better." Ralph looked at the floor, his shoulders slumping, his mind defeated.

Emma and Loren stood silently, but Ralph was glad for the support he knew they offered by being there. He couldn't look at them right now.

"How long will that be?" Nadine asked.

"Well." Ralph ventured. "It will be a long time; maybe a year or so." He knew it could be two or three but he figured they'd take it one step at a time.

Betty who was almost 13 could not imagine having Bev gone a whole year.

"How will she go to school? Who will she play with? When will we see her?"

Knowing that Betty was closest to Beverly, Ralph saw that this was not going to be an easy transition for them to make.

"We'll go and visit her, and she can come for short visits here. She'll go to the school near their house and play with kids who live around them. They don't have any children and they are going to take care of Beverly like she belonged to them."

It sounded good but he could sense that they didn't feel much better about this than he did.

"Girls, I don't know what else we can do."

Everybody sat there looking at each other. Even Betty had put down the candy that Uncle Loren had given to her.

Lynn looked at him tiredly and said, "Can we eat now?"

Ralph smiled. He figured God had sent Lynn to keep them all on track. Life would go on and they would too.

"Let's eat." Ralph said feeling stronger and he stood up next to Loren to shake his hand.

"Sure you won't join us?" Ralph hoped they knew how much he appreciated what they did because he wasn't always able to express it.

"Oh, Ralph, I've got a town council meeting tonight. We need to be on home."

Emma put her arms around Ralph, and then proceeded to give everyone a kiss. The kids always hated that but I guess it was pay back for all the candy they got. Lynn dodged good enough to get it on the ear, and then stand up on his chair and reach across to get his own cornbread.

"We'll be going down to see her on Friday." Loren said. "That is if Nadine would watch the store."

Nadine looked at Uncle Loren and Aunt Emma. "Would you really let me?"

"Would if you want to." Loren affirmed.

"Dad, can I?" Nadine would die to get a day away from the house and kids.

"I don't see why not. Darlene can take charge here at the house one day." Ralph said tiredly.

"Why can't I go to the store?" Darlene didn't want to be in charge. She was always glad to let Nadine run the show.

"You, young lady, will stay home and clean out that drawer of paper dolls so Mary can have a place to put her clothes." Ralph's look told Darlene that he meant it but wasn't really angry. She figured with Nadine gone it would give her a chance to get her stuff into a new hiding place so they wouldn't get thrown out.

"It's ok with me." Ralph said to Nadine as he pushed his chair up to the table, sat down again and pulled himself close to Lynn.

Normally he would have walked "company" out to their car, but tonight he needed to stay put. He was holding together a little circle with delicate strands of love and emotion. He knew his heart was sending up prayers of thanks and praise for the guidance he had received that day.

"We'll pick you up Thursday night." Uncle Loren was saying to Nadine.

"Be ready about 7:00."

Loren put his hat on and headed out the front door.

"Bye-bye." Emma called.

"Bye." Everybody yelled with mouths full of corn-bread and beans.

"Dad, when can we go see Beverly?" Nadine asked.

"How about Sunday? I've got some work to do tomorrow and then you're keeping the store on Friday, and Saturday I've got to haul Smith's pigs to town."

"Can I go to see Bev too?" Betty looked at him.

"We'll all go." Ralph said with confidence, feeling like he had just come through the first part of a hurricane and knowing given a short lull he could make it through the other side.

"Mary, you've got my spoon." Darlene grabbed it back.

"Well, I didn't mean to." Mary stuck out her tongue.

"Pass that cornbread and butter, Lynn." Ralph said choosing to ignore Mary's demonstration of one of her better working physical attributes.

He looked around the table at the four girls and Lynn. Bessie had blessed him, that was for sure. Even now he felt a peace. He sopped his beans up with his cornbread and took a bite. He liked hard work, and he loved his children. Little Lynn was a joy to his soul and the girls were as good as any young ladies he'd ever known. Yes, Bessie would be proud of them all that day.

He swallowed and gulped down a whole glass of milk. Leaning back he gazed across the old kitchen that he and Bessie had worked on together when they first bought the place. The cabinet painted white had been too plain for her so Bessie painted a green trim along the edge. She'd picked out the linoleum for the floors and taught the girls to braid a new rug.

Ralph gazed out the window across the big oak table that amply held them all. The pink glow of the day's heat still burned across the horizon, and maybe it was his imagination, but Ralph thought he noticed a breeze rustle the leaves of the big oak. Barn swallows zoomed around the older shed that would probably fall flat given a push in the right place, and the mooing refrain of the neighbor's cows floated softly through the air.

That's when Ralph's inner eye saw Bessie standing over near the window cooing at the baby she held in her arms. For a short time he sat there holding on to the peace of the moment. Then turning back to the present he picked up the rest of his cornbread, sopped up another bite of beans, looked around the table and smiled.

Chapter 3

Sitting on top of my belongings that were heaped together with Jack's, and resting on the soft, thick dirt, I found myself in awe of the activity taking place before me. I had a growing recognition of just how small and protected my world in Star City, Arkansas with Mama had been. Some of the men were up on the sides of the truck pulling the tarp down from where it had protected us from the sun and dusty wind that seemed to blow non-stop. They rolled the big canvas backwards, let it go, then jumped back as it fell heavily to the ground. Everyone scrambled as the dirt exploded in all directions and then began to settle upon our belongings. Though darkness was pushing the edge of the sky down behind the hills, and the pink glow of evening was about to disappear, bits of dust clinging to the moist air shimmered with reflected light from those remaining rays and it gave the sky a magical appearance.

I watched as poles were pulled from under the bed of the truck and a large lean-to was erected from the stiff and filthy tarp. Wondering if night-time protection from the elements was really worth all this effort, I was glad when the work was completed and saw that straw would be spread on the floor of the shelter before we unrolled our beds. It had been a long day. Back home we'd taken rides with Mr. Jim in his truck on Sunday afternoons when he had money for gas, but I could not remember ever riding so far or for so long at one time. Cindy, who was leaning against Cody's shoulder, looked to be sleeping. Jack had gone to "check things out" as he put it while I watched our stuff. We had eaten most of the food Mama sent, but I was feeling hungry again. Starting tomorrow morning, when we finally arrived in Iowa, we were to get our meals at the camps in exchange for the first two days labor. Shaking the dirt off our food sack, and searching deep inside of it, I discovered another piece of wrapped cornbread with some of Mama's apple butter stuck in the middle. Leaving the bigger part of it for Jack, I broke off enough to satisfy my stomach for tonight then drank the last of the water in my jar.

Sitting there, eating some of the food Mama had packed, and waiting for Jack to return, I watched to see how the arrangements for bedding down would take place. But as men began to find spots for themselves, spread out bedrolls and flop down, I came to the conclusion there were none. I looked over at Cody to see if he might be thinking the same thing. He looked at me and I knew we both understood that we'd better be getting ourselves a spot before we were left to bed on the dirt field where no straw would keep our quilts clean.

"Cindy. Wake up." Cody gently shook Cindy's shoulder and she got up looking tired and as dirty as the rest of us. "Cindy, we need to grab a spot and unroll our beds." They began to pick up their possessions just as Jack walked up.

"Well, I found the pump and the outhouses and where we will eat in the morning." He grabbed his own stuff and followed us. "This is the fairgrounds and there's a cook-shed near the well-house." Jack looked around for a moment taking in our recently constructed abode and probably wondering if it would hold until morning. "I talked to a man by the name of Parnell Walker and he said we line up there in the morning and they give us egg sandwiches and milk." Jack sounded like he was ready for breakfast already.

"There's some cornbread left in the sack for you." I told him. "But first we need to find a place for our bedrolls or we'll be out in the field on the dirt instead of the straw." And as easy as I sounded, inside I had decided that sleeping was out of the question. I was feeling as nervous as the first time Mr. Jim came to live with us. When he and Mama went to the same bedroom that first night, I worried. Sleeping in such close quarters with strange men just didn't sit right with me. It was as uncomfortable as being caught with that red rose on the backside of my drawers.

Jack grabbed the food sack and we followed Cindy and Cody, content to let them make the decision about where exactly we would position ourselves for the night. They went as far away from the others as they could get. Jack scoped out the situation, and pointed to a spot between where he was standing and where Cindy had kneeled down and was spreading out her things, insinuating that I should put my things down and make myself comfortable for the night. That suited me fine. I sure did not want to be on the edge of our group with so many men from other camps roaming around, nor did I want to be close to any of the men from our own party. Once again I was thankful that Cindy Jenkins was on this trip with us. She was placing their tote sacks neatly where pillows should have gone, next to each other as Cody stretched out his frame on the narrow pallet, then rested his head on the tote sack that Cindy had put down for him.

With an embarrassed awareness, I took in the only newly married couple I had ever been around. Of course I was around Sister and Bobby a lot before they got married, but after the ceremony, they left town. Anyway, Bobby would never be as sensitive as Cody was if he lived for a hundred years. For a man, Cody could sure be tender. I could see why Cindy fell in love with him. He seemed to sense what she felt before she even expressed it. This was not a quality I had observed in a man before. I realized I admired Cody Jenkins and was truly happy for Cindy. Those babies she wanted would be mighty lucky to be born to those two.

Jack settled down on his bed, rolled over and asked Cody if he'd seen the new picture show up in Pine Bluff. Cindy opened her tote sack and took out a towel and looked at me.

"Want to go find that pump and wash up?"

"Ok. I'll get my wash rag." I dug through my bag and pulled out what I needed and stood up. "Which way, Jack?" I asked him.

"Just follow the light on that pole." He nodded showing us the direction. Jack punched the bag under his head.

"Do you girls want an escort?" Cody offered.

"I don't know, Cody. Do you think we need one?" Cindy stood tall and lanky, and though dirty and tired like the rest of us, she still looked pretty good.

I had not been nervous about walking through the dark to the pump and outhouse, but Cody's question made me wonder. If he sensed we might have a problem other than the darkness to cope with, I wanted to know. At home I was never afraid of the dark even to go outside at night when necessary. I realized then that it was not the dark of night that created my fear, but our presence among so many men. And not just men, I thought, but married men who would be, or maybe had been away from their wives for quite awhile. I saw a few other women, but none as young as us, except some with their families. I felt anxious shivers go up my spine.

"I think I'll go with them Jack, if you'll stay with the stuff." Cody hopped up and grabbed Cindy's hand. "Let's go."

"See ya." Jack waved, rolled onto his back, and closed his eyes. I was relieved to have Cody go with us and angry at Jack for not being more concerned.

I wondered if Cody had a special sense about the responsibilities of being a married man that Jack did not possess. I wondered if the feelings and needs of married men were different than those of a single man. Men were confusing creatures, and I felt too tired to try and come to any conclusions about them tonight. I was confident that I needed to stay alert, and very nervous about the prospect of any confrontation. We walked as Jack had directed us.

The night was warm and humid. I hoped to get off the layers of dust we had accumulated but could see no end to the sweat rolling down the small of my back or the back of my knees. Insects buzzed louder as we neared the dim electric light pole. I saw the hand pump, the cook-shed and the privy at opposite ends of the area. Cindy and I followed a well worn path to the pump and found a bucket already full of water under the faucet. We dipped our rags in and began to wash. It was cold and felt good in spite of the fact that I felt timid about this method of public washing. What I really wanted to do was to jump right in and soak, but I managed to get fairly clean without giving in to any ten year old yearnings. Cindy and I dusted each other's clothes off and then brushed out our hair. I was glad that mine was short because it meant less to get dirty and the hat covered most of it keeping the dirt from my scalp. Cindy's pony tail was dull looking, but hopefully, when we reached Iowa there would be a place to really bathe.

Cody stood off from us talking to a man about his experiences following the harvest. Either he sensed my shyness or Cindy had informed him about it because he was certainly making this easier than it could have been for me. At home, grooming, and especially bathing had been a very private matter, even between my brothers and sisters. I wondered if life would ever be the same again for me. Never before feeling so much uncertainty, I was sure my eyes revealed the fear that was creeping up from the depths of my soul.

"Want to walk to the outhouse, now?" Cindy asked me.

"Sure," I returned, knowing I was not about to get up during the night to go.

"We'll be right back, Cody." Cindy called to him. He waved and nodded at us but continued to listen to the man he had met there and who was talking in that slow drawn out whine of a voice that Jack referred to as "hillbilly" talk.

I looked back over my shoulder to see if Cody was

keeping one eye on us as we took the little path that left the small circle of light shining from the pole by the pump.

"Are you ok?" Cindy asked not looking at me but down at the path that led the way.

"I'm a little nervous about spending the night so near all those men we don't know." Actually I was more than a little nervous but I tried to appear grown up. "What about you?" I could not see her eyes, but knew they reflected my own growing distrust of the situation.

"I didn't like the way that one man kept looking at us today in the truck. Did you notice?" Cindy stopped just outside of the door to the toilet.

"What?" I asked, fear suddenly griping me. Questions raced through my mind. What man? How was he looking? How could I not have noticed? If I wasn't unsettled before, I was now.

"I'm sorry. I didn't mean to upset you so, but that man who was wearing the brown cowboy hat kept looking sideways out of his eyes towards us all afternoon. I pretended I didn't notice and I didn't say anything to Cody because I figured it would just cause a problem and we should be in Iowa by tomorrow night. But watch out for him, Johnnie Belle. You know how men can be. Even if they're married they can act like they're not." Cindy's soft expression was sisterly and reminded me of Sister.

A wave of homesickness breezed through me. I wanted familiarity; Mama, Harold, Sister or even Mr. Jim. I did not want to be here. Anger began to stir and I decided it was Jack's fault. It was Jack's fault that I was here and hot and dirty and tired and scared.

"I'll go in first." Cindy said, probably hoping to give me time to absorb what she had told me and give her time to figure out how to respond to the feelings she could certainly read on my face. I waited letting my anger at Jack mount almost into tears. When Cindy came out I did not look at her but took my turn in the little shed. By the time I came out, I looked directly at Cindy, and lost every attempt I'd made to be mature.

"Cindy," I said tensely through tears not trying to hide my feelings of misery. "I really just want to go back home." I took a shaky breath. "You see, Jack and Mama want me to get on with my life and I got talked into this. I've got to grow up someday, but this is more than I counted on. I'm afraid I didn't think this trip through at all. I can't let Jack down now by asking him to take me back to Star City, and I would be too afraid of going back alone." Forbidden tears escaped my eyes and streamed down my face. "I don't know what to do." I looked away from Cindy, and took a big breath trying to calm myself. Cindy stared wide-eyed at me probably shocked both with the state I was in and my non-stop dribble.

"This is all so complicated and confusing." I continued. "I mean, I'm scared of the men, but I'm scared too that Jack and Cody and those men will see that I'm scared. My mind is spinning with so many new things to deal with and I'm so tired." My hands were in a clench and I was gripping the wet rags close to my shirt and the dampness aggravated my misery. I felt helpless.

Seeing me break down after a long tiring day under stressful circumstances, she put her arm around me and gripped my shoulders tightly. I could almost feel some release of the tension that had built.

"Johnnie Belle, let's you and me be like sisters. I know I've got Cody and he's just as good as they come, but there's nothing like having a good girlfriend to confide in. You've got to learn to let out your feelings. I miss my own sister and I need you as much as you need me."

Cindy stood hugging me waiting for an answer. My anger with Jack began to fade just a little. She had moved quickly from shock over my sudden dismay, to a mothering/sisterly mode. It worked. I guess having sisters of her own had given her both wisdom and experience in dealing with a girl's perspective on life.

I nodded my head managing a smile. "You're right. I just feel so tired right now."

I was a little embarrassed, but mostly about letting my fears take control. "Cindy." I stammered. "I'm sorry to be so silly and immature. I'm afraid that I didn't really have much of an idea about what I was getting myself in for coming with Jack. He's adventurous and courageous. You must wonder how I could be so stupid."

"Hardly," Cindy sounded surprised. "When I first found out that a single girl would be on the truck, I admired every bone in your body. Why, I am proud to be your friend, Johnnie Belle. And, I'm glad you're here. I miss my sisters so much."

It was the first time, I think, I'd ever been through a crisis without someone from my family there by my side. As Cindy and I stood there in the night, emotionally clinging to each other, I knew that she did need me as much as I needed her. Together we had taken a step of confidence. This road we were on held dangers and a lot of unknowns, but I recognized that I had just come through one episode, and that I could find my way through others because I had a friend.

Cindy smiled, linked her arm in mine and we headed back down the path towards where Cody was now involved in conversation with four other fellows. Our walk was somewhat courageous but more of a resolve to the friendship we'd found in womanly companionship and our attempt at survival in a man's world.

Cody looked up at us, nodded to the men surrounding him acknowledging his end to the discussion and he joined us in our walk back to the camp. He walked a pace behind us, possibly sensing the bond Cindy and I had formed and allowing us space to share an intimacy that did not include him.

Leaving the circle of light that surrounded that gathering spot for those not willing to give up the day, I tried to peer through the darkness for a count of other shelters, but I couldn't see a thing. Thinking that it might be better to not know how many camps surrounded us, I relaxed and decided I needed to think about being sensible instead of fearful. I began to hear Mama's voice telling me to get my bearings on where I was and who was around so I could take care of myself. I realized now that she knew what I might be facing and had talked to me over the last few weeks about how to cope. At the time I did not realize what she meant, but now I did. She knew that I'd think about her words when the time came and I struggled for wisdom.

Smiling to myself, I owned up to the fact that I was still not really making it on my own. But that was ok. Mama would be an influence the rest of my life. Nobody ever dealt with life truly alone. We all carry the voices of others who have experienced life in front of us and who turn around to tell us about adventures yet to come. Funny how at the time we barely listen, but later as we face our own experiences, those voices drift from the past and help to shape the present.

I let my mind drift back to those evenings the last few weeks at home. Thinking about it now, Mama did spend more time with me than usual. I remember how we'd sit on the porch mending or stand in the kitchen putting up soup with any vegetables we could scrounge and Mama would talk about things. At the time I didn't think she was really talking to me. I just listened as I always did. Now her voice floated across the miles and through my head giving me comfort.

We got close to our camp, and Jack jumped up. He must have been watching for us.

"If you guys are back for awhile, I need to fill our water jars and wash up myself." He looked as if he'd waited just about as long as he could. There was no patience in that boy!

"Sure," Cody said. "Take as much time as you want. I think the ladies are done for the night and I'm fine."

"Ok with you, Johnnie Belle?" Jack asked to be sure.

"Yes. I'm fine." I replied. "Now," I thought.

"Where'd you get your name from Johnnie Belle?" Cindy asked as we both settled down on our bed rolls between Cody and Jack's pallets.

"Mama said it was a name she'd heard before I was born and she liked the sound of it. I guess I'm used to it because it feels like it belongs to me, if you know what I mean."

"I do," said Cindy. "My parents always call me Cindy Lou, but at school they just called me Cindy. Cindy seems more grown up sounding but I like it when Mama calls me Cindy Lou."

"Are you homesick?" I asked quietly.

"More than I try to think about." Cindy looked at me, then rolled onto her stomach and cradled her chin in her arms. "I miss my sisters and of course the baby. It's hard not even knowing how things are going there."

"Let's get some postcards and write the first chance we get, Cindy." I remembered I'd promised Mama that I would write.

"That's a good idea, Johnnie Belle." Cindy looked at me.

I plumped up my sack to use as a pillow.

"Do you see him?" She whispered as though she did not want Cody to hear her.

I looked at her face and then around the tent realizing that she was talking about the man from the truck with the brown cowboy hat that had stared at us today.

"I'm not sure." I said. "I sure don't want to stare back and most of them have their hats off. It's too dark to see really. Are you scared?"

"Not too much, but I think we should pay attention from now on and not get caught too close to him or too far from the boys." Cindy closed her eyes.

"It's funny isn't it that you can sit down and do nothing all day but ride and still feel so tired. I guess it's the heat." I lay down next to Cindy on my quilt.

I could not decide which was worse, the stillness of the humid air or the waves of dry wind that we had dealt with all day. I was sweating again so I lay still and closed my eyes as well. I heard Jack come up from the darkness and put our water jars beside the beds. He lay down on his own blanket and sighed.

"Everything ok here?" he asked.

"Fine," I said. Things were getting quiet. I could hear men off in the distance playing cards, serenaded by a harmonica and a fiddle or maybe two. Listening to the music, I relaxed.

"I'm going to walk to the outhouse, Jack." I heard Cody say softly. Then I felt him kneel down to Cindy's side and whisper that he'd be right back.

My eyes opened and I saw her lift up enough to give him a quick kiss, then lay back down. For the first time in my life I was willing to admit to myself that one day I wanted to be married to a man who really loved me. I wanted a man who made me feel like I belonged with him and not to him. I thought about that as I rolled over onto my stomach. Knowing we had an early morning, and feeling safe with Jack beside me, I closed my eyes. I couldn't think of a one boy I had known who met my qualifications. It did not, however, worry me or keep me awake.

My dreams took me back home to my own bed where my old doll lay on top of the new quilt Mama made when I was thirteen. She said that it was a quilt for a grown girl because it told a story about a woman's life. Then she told me about all the different blocks she'd sewn and how each one represented another step in my life. One was a wedding ring pattern. At the time I pretended the circles were two faces, mine and some boy I would marry. An unknown, faceless man somewhere out there in the big wide world. Some man waiting for me to find him, to be his wife. I stared at the blank face in my dream. Suddenly a hole opened up right in the center of the quilt and formed into a sickly smile. The little face began to talk slowly and with a slurred voice like a drunk. I watched as the face became almost real and formed into a head. I looked up to see Mama floating away until she was sucked into the blackness. The face just kept smiling eerily and the lips kept moving with a voice that was far away. I felt afraid as though I could not escape. Then in a flash it disappeared. My body jerked. I opened my eyes and everything was dark. I realized that I was no longer at home, and I'd been dreaming. I was awake here in the camp, under a shelter, and bedded down on straw. But for some reason far off in the distance I could still hear the drunken voice of the face from my dream.

I was trying to shake the eerie feeling of the dream state I had been pulled from while at the same time trying to find the self-control to figure out what was going on and why I could still hear the sickly slur of that voice. I tried to breathe evenly and stay calm. The air was thick and I heard a bug buzzing in my ear. I listened too afraid to move. The sound of the man was getting closer to our camp and I could hear him singing in a quiet drunken rhythm that had no words. From farther across the field the trickle of deep male voices droned off and on in low conversation, but the music had stopped.

Every so often a few whoops of laughter peeled through the dark as if someone playing cards had just been dealt a winning hand. I knew from experience, however, that most of that laughter was most likely embellished by drink. I was hopeful that those men were from a camp different than ours. Lying still, I was afraid to move let alone raise Jack. The fear I felt, increased as the voice of the drunken man got closer. Apparently, Jack, Cindy, and Cody had not been awakened because they were all breathing softly and unmoving. I figured it was better to pretend to be asleep. Laying on my side and watching the direction of the sound, my eyes had adjusted enough to see a man approaching the very corner the four of us had chosen as a haven. The man staggered across the straw floor and fell close to where we had settled. I gasped. He lay still and the smell of his libations was clear enough to inform me that he was probably there for the duration of the night. I wondered how long I had slept and how much longer it would be until the sun came up again. I lay still, wanting nothing but my home, my bed, and Mama. I did not feel like a woman at all, but a mere child who yearned for comfort.

My eyes would not close. They were not to be pried from the heap of filth that had crumbled close enough to touch with my foot if I extended it far enough. Tension bound my body. I told myself that he was out and I was safe from any harm. Numb from the exhaustion of the trip, emotional distress and the inability to sleep, I gazed beyond the edge of the tarp at the stars. My mind refused to process any thought, and relaxation was apparently not within my grasp. The beauty of the sky slowly enveloped me and I pretended to float among the twinkling bits of fire. Somewhere between the moon and the morning, I blinked my eyes and thought I heard Jack calling my name. The light of the new day cleansed the fear from my mind and my breath was deep and calm. I looked over and saw Jack sitting on his bed. I knew he had waited as long as he could before he woke me.

"Johnnie Belle, wake up."

"Ok," was all I could manage and I pulled myself up,

reached for a brush and then remembered the man. I glanced to the foot of our beds and there was no man there. Jack eyed me.

"I roused him earlier and sent him packing." He said.

"I thought maybe it was a dream." I spoke mostly to myself.

"Lots of men get away from their wives and families and lose any sense they ever had." Jack knew I understood. I just sat there for a moment thinking back over my dream and decided to put it behind me.

I looked over at Cindy who was sleeping curled up in Cody's arms, then back at Jack. He smiled at me and I smiled back. I'm not sure exactly what we were thinking but it was probably close to the same thing. We headed to the outhouses together and then stood in line for breakfast.

Heading back towards the tent our hands full of hot egg sandwiches, Jack and I ran into Cody and Cindy.

"Hey you guys. Good morning, Johnnie Belle." Cody shook Jack's free hand and nodded his head at me. I smiled back.

"The breakfast is pretty good and filling." Jack said.

"Morning, Johnnie Belle. Did you sleep well?" Cindy asked.

"I don't think so," I said with a smile. "But, there's always tonight." I wanted her to know that I felt stronger today and I was not calling it quits just yet.

Cody put his arm around Cindy. "We'll get ourselves a bite and meet you back at the camp."

"Ok." Jack waved. "Johnnie Belle, let's get our gear rolled up. Maybe I can help take the lean-to down and roll it back onto the truck." Jack sounded ready for some physical exercise and I was sure he was. I was ready for a nap, but guess I had all day to get it in.

Men were everywhere. I could see what looked like about 20 camps of different sizes. There were a few families with children who looked like they had packed every thing they owned on their trucks and were moving for good. I wasn't sure how some of the old cars held all their belongings and the families too. Life must be hard to have to move your whole family across country, but the drought had done some terrible things to so many people. I'd read the stories in the old newspapers that Mama brought home. They talked about people who ate under blankets to keep from having dirt blow right into their food, and showed pictures of the dust storms that would last for days and moving from state to state. Farmers told about cattle starving and children dying from just breathing in all that dirt.

We got back to our group, finished our breakfast and rolled our beds after shaking the dirt and straw back into the ground. We piled our things under a tree and I told Jack I'd stay near that tree while he talked to the men about helping to tear down the canvas and reassemble it as protection over the truck bed. I leaned against the big trunk and watched a family with a girl about thirteen and a boy about ten, eat some bread for their breakfast. People all over were packing up. I guess everyone had an idea of a better place to go. I wondered if there really was a better place to go or if it was just a false hope. For once I thought seriously about what we were doing. I thought about Jack trying to make enough money to get married. Then I thought about myself and my life. Up to now this trip had been an adventure that I had undertaken to please others. Now I decided that I needed to formulate a plan for my own life. Was I going to work with Jack and when he went back to Arkansas go with him? Would I make some money then go to a city and find a place to live and a job there? What would I do? I wondered what kind of jobs I'd find in a city. I could work in a store. I could sew and clean. I had no idea about how anybody would go into a city and find any job. Feeling overwhelmed again I sat down.

"Hello, Johnnie Belle." I heard Cindy call to me.

"Hello, Cindy." I waved, smiling. "Bring your stuff over here and sit with me."

I got up and went over to help her. We leaned their bedrolls and tote sacks against the tree. Cody went over to where Jack was talking to a group of men. Cindy and I stood near the tree, both of us anticipating a long day sitting on a bench.

"Cindy, have you ever been to a city?" I asked.

"I went to Little Rock once with my family." Cindy said. "My Daddy thought we should see the capitol." She paused remembering back.

"How would you get a job in a city?" I asked.

"I remember my sister once got a newspaper and read about jobs. She read about different work in different places and how much money they paid." She looked at me. "Why?"

"Well, when Jack goes back to Arkansas I might have to go to a city and look for a job." I responded calmly hiding my uncertainty and fear of the unknown.

"Oh, Johnnie Belle, that sounds scary. I mean where would you live and you wouldn't know anybody." Cindy looked at me like she could hardly believe I was even thinking about this. I was glad to hear the same feelings I'd been having.

"What else will I do? There's nothing for me to do back in Star City. There is no boy I'm interested in. There's sure no place to work. I guess a girl can't live with her Mama all her life." It wasn't as though I really believed what I was saying, but more of trying to convince myself of what was expected of me. I watched as Jack and Cody helped lower the lean-to and begin to roll the heavy tarp back up. Dust swirled around in the dry wind. I wiped my face with my sleeve.

"What do you want to do?" Cindy looked at me.

"I liked living at home with my family. I liked helping around the house and working in the garden and taking care of my younger brother." I remembered the garden we'd had this year and how bad it was. "I can cook and clean and sew."

"What about book work and reading and 'rithmetic?" Cindy went on. "Are you good at that?"

"Well," I thought for a minute. "I like to read and I'm pretty good at it. I can do sums and times in my head."

"Besides, housework, you might work for a business man or in a factory where they sew clothes." Cindy looked like she was trying to think about me working for a business man.

I laughed. "I don't know about that. I don't think I'd like to be cooped up all day inside." I saw the men getting the sides of the tarp strapped down on the truck and the poles tied back underneath the truck. Someone had the hood up and was pouring water in the front of the engine. I did not know a thing about motors that was for sure.

"I think we should find you a nice man, Johnnie Belle." Cindy said.

"Well, I don't know for sure about that." I retorted.

Cindy laughed and we got up and began to pick up our things. It was still early but our group looked ready to be on the road. The leader was waving everyone around him so we drifted over to where Cody and Jack were standing to hear what he had to say.

The man waited a minute for every one to quiet down. "We got a long ride today cause we be a goin' all the way to Shenandoah."

Cindy and I looked at each other with determination after the experience of one day on the road. We'd both grown up more in that one day than either of us had ever expected. At this rate I figured I'd be an old woman faster than Mama.

We got in the line to load our belongings and ourselves. No one seemed to be in a hurry to get back into the frame that would carry us another twelve to fifteen hours across the state of Missouri and into Iowa.

I looked behind me where Jack was carrying his own load and glanced across the field. Coming toward the end of the line was a man wearing an old brown cowboy hat. His tired unshaven face was scarred and made him appear angry. I turned back to where Cindy and Cody were moving ahead of me toward the back of the truck. I focused on the plan I needed to form for moving on with my life. I tried to think of what I was good at. I knew Jack was right behind me.

Chapter 4

Ralph Abraham Showalter stood before the dim mirror in the kitchen, across from the stove, and slowly began to shave the dark growth from his face being careful not to nick his skin. He grew up with the habit of looking his best on Sunday mornings and it had stayed with him. It wasn't that Ralph did not shave on other days but rarely did he slow down enough to actually study his own reflection and make the effort to appear to be a gentleman. With so many responsibilities, his mind was usually beyond the task at hand and thinking through the chores that lay before him.

He had also grown up in a family that did not work on Sundays. This was another habit that he held to. For some reason, though, he was not as good at stifling the thoughts that fired through his head as he was at slowing down his body. It was not easy to shake the awareness of ideas that nervously waited their turn on the edge of his consciousness. It was as if there was no end to the pieces of information to be sorted through, panicked over, or filed away. Sometimes his brain raced like a tornado, out of control, flying and spinning, upending ideas and plans that had already been laid or developing new ones. It took an effort on Ralph's part to stymie all that thinking into organized patterns so it could be dwelled upon as needed. If it wasn't the children, the house, his father, the car or truck, his trucking contacts and schedules, it was something else. And now Beverly's illness was added to the parade of thoughts that wanted time from him. Often he doubted that he made any progress at all as life marched by one day at a time.

Ralph looked in the mirror examining his olive skin, made darker from the sun. He knew some people thought he was good looking. He combed his dark hair that naturally parted down the middle and observed his nose. Though it was considered large, it fit his face and his lean six-foot frame. Hard work and the worries of the children had aged his soul, but physically his body was in top shape. He dropped the comb on the wash-stand below the mirror, beside the razor, and went to put on his shirt. In his mind he had a vision of how he looked in his Sunday clothes and without guilt, anticipated the attention that always came to him upon his family's arrival at Sharp's Grove Methodist Church each week. Ralph never sought attention purposefully, but he enjoyed it all the same. Occasionally he even flirted with the women who flaunted their wiles at him, though never seriously, and that's probably the reason it continued.

He was currently considered the local "catch," and it was no mystery. In this small community, there were few men his age who weren't married, and in a day when big families were the norm, even having seven children was not necessarily an encumbrance. Emma, his sister, thought he should court Elizabeth Yates. Her husband died last year leaving her with two small children of her own. Elizabeth was plenty nice and good looking enough, but Ralph just did not have time to pursue romance. When he got home at night, he wanted and needed to spend the time with his children, and then he was simply too tired to go out again. Ralph pulled on his pants and then his shoes.

"Girls," he yelled. "Are you about ready to go?"

"Daddy, I can't find my ribbon for my dress," Mary answered.

"I told you to look in your drawer." Nadine yelled coming in from the outhouse.

"I found it!" Mary yelled back.

Ralph knew that if he remained quiet long enough the girls usually settled their squabbles themselves. They learned soon enough after Bessie died that he was not much help when it came to getting girls dressed. Being raised mostly by his

Father after his own Mother's death had caused him to be a little rough around the edges no matter how hard he tried. Women were different creatures than men, and he was living proof of that.

"Lynn, are you cleaned up from breakfast, yet?" Ralph asked of the five year old who was standing at the picture window watching some birds in the front yard.

"Yes, Daddy." Lynn hollered as he ran out the front door letting the screen door slam.

Ralph tried to remember how old the girls were before they no longer slammed a screen door.

"Dad, Darlene didn't throw away those paper dolls. I saw them in a sack, under the bed." Betty tattled.

Ralph looked at Betty. She looked more like him than the others, her olive skin, dark hair and eyes and lean frame.

"Betty, are you ready to go to church?" He asked, ignoring her remark.

"Yes, but can I wear that hat of Mama's?"

"I guess if you don't tear it up," Ralph replied remembering Bessie in that hat she wore every Sunday morning.

"I won't," Betty said as she went into the bedroom that had been his and Bessie's before she died. Betty took it off the nail in the wall where Ralph had let it hang.

"Lynn, head to the car." Ralph yelled through the screen, then headed toward the back door. He just could not get used to using the front door even on Sunday.

"Nadine, Mary, Darlene let's go." Ralph made his way outside and looked up to see if there was any bit of breeze at all. He couldn't feel it but he thought the leaves moved some. He felt tired as he headed for their car noticing Ralph Wendell had made it home from town last night. He opened the front door and helped Lynn to crawl up under the steering wheel and over to the middle of the seat. He sat down but did not close the car door because he knew that Darlene would take awhile to get out the door and it was already hot.

"Daddy, can I drive?" Lynn asked crawling up on Ralph's lap and playing with the wheel.

"We'll see." Ralph used that answer most often. It put off telling him no which meant it put off hearing him yell. He'd done a good job giving in to Lynn one too many times. Since he had taken Lynn on his trucking trips so often, Lynn acted more like an only child who got his way most of the time. Ralph had a mild temperament and Lynn survived his tantrums only because of this.

Nadine and Mary came out the front door, followed by Betty. They got into the back seat with Betty in the middle. Then came Darlene. She ambled around the car and got in the front seat beside Lynn. Amusedly, Darlene appeared to be in her own world. Ralph pushed Lynn off his lap and sat him in the middle next to Darlene. Ralph recognized that Darlene had his personality. Sometimes he new exactly what she was thinking. Nothing seemed to get her ire up, and she was able to ignore Nadine when Nadine got in her Motherly mode. Ralph started up the old car and pulled out of the yard. He thought about Beverly. He missed her. She would usually sit between Mary and Nadine with Betty. Those two little ones seemed to get along so well.

"I'm so hot! Betty, scoot over some." Nadine was growing up and did not like the younger ones to get her dirty when she had her Sunday best on.

"Daddy, did you hear me tell you that Darlene did not get rid of her paper dolls, because I found them under the bed this morning when I was looking for my Sunday shoes." Mary said righteously. "Are you going to make her throw them away?"

Mary sounded like Nadine. Ralph guessed she was in

training to take over Nadine's job of running the household when Nadine left for school. He wondered if it was an unconscious effort to try and fill Bessie's role as Nadine had done. Wondering if Mary was scared to be losing Nadine he decided he should talk to her about it. Ralph looked at Darlene across the front seat and over Lynn's head. Darlene looked back at him.

"I found a place for them and it won't hurt anybody. Nobody needs that space under our bed and the sack wasn't in use." Darlene spoke frankly and looking directly into his eyes. She knew that he would understand and he did.

Ralph looked at her again not saying anything, knowing that Mary would reply and the debate would continue if he just gave it enough time.

"But, Dad, you told her to throw them out." Mary did not let him down.

Ralph sighed and looked over at Darlene again as he drove out of the yard and down the dirt road. There was definitely a breeze picking up and with it the dirt swirled into the windows. He drove a little faster. Ralph liked speed when he was alone but tried to be more careful when the children were with him. Ignoring the previous question he considered that he needed to teach Nadine to drive before she left for Chillicothe and business school. He had about two months.

"Nadine, you need to get out in the car this week and learn to drive." Ralph said. He figured that driving wasn't hard and she could probably do it without too much instruction. Maybe he could get Ralph Wendell to stay home long enough to teach her.

"OK," was all Nadine said. Her mind was probably on that young Jacobs, boy she'd had her eye on at church.

"Don't you want to learn?" Ralph asked thinking she'd have shown a little more excitement. Of course, once again, he was thinking like a man.

.

"Well, yes, I guess I do." Nadine said warily.

Ralph sensed that maybe she was a little bit scared.

"Nadine, Mrs. Baxter has a car and when you stay with her she wants your help to drive her around." The older woman had been like a Mother to him and Bessie when they first got married. Now she was helping them again by taking in Nadine while she went to school, but this time he'd been able to offer the help of Nadine in exchange. Mrs. Baxter did not get around like she used to and, with her husband gone, she did need someone to stay with her and help her out. Ralph knew that Nadine would be as good for Mrs. Baxter as Mrs. Baxter would be for Nadine.

"Can I learn too?" Darlene asked.

Ralph looked at her wondering. Darlene was not as forward as Mary was and she didn't usually pursue the unknown unless there was a good reason for it. He wondered what she had up her sleeve.

"I don't see why not," Ralph said. "Might as well teach you both."

Ralph put that thought at the end of the line of thoughts that were lined up waiting for some action to be taken and pushed his Sunday straw hat back on his head.

Turning down the little lane that led to the church, the dust puffed behind their car. He looked in his mirrors and knew when he stopped it would fly into the car and all over their clothes. He slowed evenly until as he reached the church yard he was at a crawl. He parked beside Joe Smith's truck and turned off the key. The girls were piling out before the tires had stopped rolling. They all took off to meet up with their friends and to get the seats near the back of the church. Ralph let them all go except for Lynn who ran over to the Meyer's little boy, about his same age. Ralph felt a catch in his throat remembering Bessie and Joanne being so big with the babies, all at the same time. He waved and smiled and saw

Elizabeth Yates and her two young'uns stalling at the front door of the church.

He walked over to the Meyer's and joined them as they approached the steps that led up to the shabby white doors that reminded him about the much needed paint job.

Ralph had attended church here since he was born. The Tharp family had long ago donated the land and the cemetery had been named after them. Later they built the little church and named it Sharp's Grove Church. He never understood why they didn't just call it the Tharp's Grove Church to match the cemetery, but he figured there was some reason. Elizabeth and her boys went on in, followed by the Meyer's family and then Ralph and Lynn. Since church was close to starting, Elizabeth Yates quickly chose a pew and the Meyer's followed her in which filled it up. Ralph had no choice but to sit behind them causing him to grin. He knew that Elizabeth was making a play to sit with him. He pulled Lynn by the hand and they sat down. She looked over her shoulder and smiled. Ralph smiled back. He knew he was a flirt and felt just a little bit guilty for it.

Lynn squirmed around for the first part of the service then settled down and leaned against Ralph's arm and closed his eyes. Ralph pulled his arm around his little shoulders and hugged him close to his own body. It wasn't long before Lynn leaned into his lap asleep. Ralph envied his repose as the preacher droned on.

Keeping his mind on the sermon today was harder than ever because he was thinking about Beverly and their trip to St. Joseph that afternoon. Finally they stood for the last hymn and Ralph picked up Lynn and put his sleeping head over his shoulder. Ralph liked singing and had always encouraged music with his girls. His wasn't shy about letting his voice resound in the little sanctuary and Elizabeth once again smiled at him from her pew. He nodded his head at her but continued singing through the last amen.

As they filed down the isle of the church and out the front doors into the sunlight and hot wind, Ralph looked for the girls. He saw them huddled near the car. The light caught Lynn's eyes and he lifted his head up from the padding of the suit that had served so well as a pillow, frowned then put his head back down. Elizabeth Yates walked up behind them.

"Hello Ralph," she said. "How is Beverly?"

"Better," Ralph looked at her not really wanting to discuss the situation of Beverly living with the Doctor, but realizing it would be known sooner or later.

"Are you going to St. Joe today?" She picked up one of her little ones as Ralph let Lynn slide down to stand on his own two legs.

"After dinner we're all going down. The kids miss her and she misses them." Ralph let go of Lynn's hand as he steadied his stance.

"Tell the girl's I'll bring dinner over on Wednesday." Elizabeth said.

"You don't have to do that Elizabeth." Ralph replied. "They can get supper on just fine."

"I know," Elizabeth looked at him and put her hand on his arm, "But I also know that once in awhile teen-age girls get tired of cooking dinner."

"Thank you," Ralph looked at her, not liking to take charity, but knowing that she was right, and then, not entirely unscathed by her touch, admitted to himself that any ulterior motives Elizabeth had were not entirely unappreciated. "We'll look forward to it. See you then." He turned and headed toward the car.

"Let's go girls," he said before he got there.

"Daddy, Ann Preston asked me to spend the night tonight. Can I?" Betty had run over to him and was looking up grinning the sun out of her eyes.

She was so cute. "Sure, but tell them it will be later tonight that I'll drop you off because we're going to the hospital."

"Thanks Daddy." Betty ran off to where Ann was getting in the car with her own family. Ralph watched her go and then returned and jumped into the back seat. Mary was waiting on one side, Nadine on the other. Both girls climbed into the big car and slammed the doors. Lynn crawled across the steering wheel and Darlene got into the front side. Some things never changed. Ralph started up the car and they headed for home.

Pulling into the drive and parking in the yard, Ralph studied the old shed that was close to the house. Before the summer was over, he would get Ralph Wendell to help him fix it before it fell in. It made a good garage for the car before it took to leaning. He left the car in gear and turned off the ignition.

"Let's get some dinner," he said, "And head to St. Joe before it gets late."

The girls sauntered lazily into the house probably none too eager to be the first to change clothes and have to work in the kitchen. Lynn ran to the swing. Ralph headed in towards his bedroom to change out of his own Sunday clothes.

"Dad, would you tell Mary to hang up her dress. Last week she left it in a pile on the floor until Wednesday." Nadine yelled as she passed his bedroom door on her way to the kitchen.

Ralph opened his door and went to the bottom of the narrow stairs that led to the girls room. "Girls hang up your clothes and get down here and help Nadine." He figured that if Mary needed yelling at then probably they all needed it. By yelling "girls" he thought he could take care of all of them at once. He was not very good at discipline so it was a good thing Bessie had raised them to be as good as they were.

Walking to the kitchen he got a broom and decided to sweep the back porch. The thought to clean did not occur to Ralph very often. Once in awhile he thought about helping out in the house and sweeping was something he knew how to do. In reality, Ralph did not notice things like dirty floors or dishes. When he was growing up, boys worked outside and he received little exposure to the household side of daily chores, so it wasn't very often he got upset if things were left undone. He simply did not notice. When he did think about it though, he tried to show the girls that everyone, even Dad, could be helpful.

Nadine watched as her Dad came into the kitchen to get the broom. She wondered what possessed him occasionally to try to help out in the house. She had to smile to herself because whatever he did usually did not make much difference, but she guessed it made him feel like he was helping out. She got dinner on the table and Darlene came in and set out the plates and silverware, then went to fill the glasses with milk.

Mary walked into the kitchen.

"Mary, did you hang up your dress?" Ralph asked.

"Yes." She looked at Nadine. "Tattletale."

"Well, if you'd do what you're supposed to I wouldn't have to tell Dad to make you." Nadine said sounding more like Bessie every day.

Ralph didn't like to hear the girls bickering and he was glad Mary did not continue in that direction. "Is dinner ready?"

"Yes." Nadine answered.

"Let's eat." Ralph yelled out the window at Lynn. He assumed the girls upstairs heard him too since he had a voice that carried itself well.

Dinner went quickly and the family once again

climbed into their places in the car and headed for St. Joseph. The wind blew through the windows and though it was hot and dry it was better than nothing. The girls did not mind the wind in their hair since they kept it braided and tied up anyway - something their mother had taught them to do in the summers. Aunt Ruth would trim it up when needed, but Ralph went to the barber every Saturday. It was part of his Sunday cleaning up ritual, hair cuts, shining shoes and hanging out the good clothes.

The kids were quiet knowing that the trip took two hours and Lynn was already sleeping across Darlene's lap. He new Betty would be the next one out. He looked over his shoulder at her already leaning toward Mary and her eyes in a daze.

Ralph thought about Beverly. Though he wished more than anything it did not have to be, he was getting used to the idea that she was not coming home. He knew that in the next few weeks they would have to pack up her clothes and take them to the Doctor's house and see where she was to live. The Doc was a nice enough fellow but his wife was formal and made him feel uncomfortable. Ralph wondered if Beverly would end up a city girl.

Seeing the houses of St. Joseph before him brought Ralph out of his thoughts and back to the present. He nudged Lynn and told him they were there, giving him time to wake up. Driving through the streets of town, Ralph headed in the direction of the hospital. He could have driven it in his sleep.

"There it is." He said as he pulled into a parking lot and lined his car up with the others parked neatly in rows. Once again he turned the ignition off but this time he pulled the keys out and put them into his pocket. He did not want to come back here and find that someone had decided to borrow his car. The girls got out and stretched.

The hospital was built of dark brick and did not look like a fun or happy place. They were all quiet as they followed their Dad across the street and into the front lobby, each of them alone in their own thoughts which ranged from their Mother, their loss of her, and now, Beverly's illness. Time had not yet healed the wounds life had given them.

Going to the elevator, Ralph led the procession up to the third floor and down a hall. He ignored the sour looks given him by two nurses. Children usually weren't allowed but Doc had given him special permission and it was visiting hours.

Beverly was in a ward shared by three other young girls, one that Ralph had not seen before. Beverly was sitting up in her bed playing with a doll. She looked up and grinned with surprise when she saw them all. Her pale face became almost glowing. Ralph could see the improvement and was thankful.

"Betty! Mary! Nadine! Darlene! Lynn!" It was as if she could not believe they were all there and she had to say their names to make it true.

The girls all hugged her but Lynn held back shy to find his sister in this strange place. Ralph picked up Lynn and put him on Beverly's bed. Beverly grabbed him and gave him a hug and a kiss.

"That's what Aunt Emma does!" They all laughed.

"How do you feel today?" Ralph went over to the other side of her bed.

"Better. I want to go home, Daddy." Her lower lip trembled remembering that she would not be leaving to go home to the farm, but to the Doctor's house.

"Do I still have to go to Doc Miller's house?" Beverly looked at him with dread in her eyes.

"Yes." He said looking away so maybe she would not notice his sadness.

"Daddy said we'd still get to see you sometimes and

you could come home for short visits." Nadine said with a motherly tone.

"We can write letters." Darlene told her.

"You know they're probably rich and you won't have to do any dishes." Mary told her with a little bit of envy.

Betty didn't say anything and looked like she was about to cry.

"Betty, will you come and visit me?" Beverly looked at her.

"Can I, Daddy?" Betty looked up at her father.

"We'll see if she can go for a visit before the month's over." He smiled sadly at his little girls.

Beverly got out of bed and went to the end of the ward where there were a few toys, games and puzzles. Lynn began to play with a truck. The girls sat on the floor and talked and played with Beverly's doll while Ralph sat in an old rocking chair and watched his children. He felt calmed by the quiet of the ward, the soft voices of the children, and the easy manner in which they played together. Nadine picked up a story book and began to read it aloud. She sat cross legged. Lynn crawled up on one side of Nadine while Beverly leaned against her on the other side. Darlene was reading a book silently by herself and Mary and Betty still played with the doll. As Lynn listened, he rolled his truck back and forth on the floor.

After a time, a nurse came in with Beverly's supper tray. Ralph looked at his watch and realized how late it had gotten.

"Time to go." He announced noticing that Beverly looked tired. "Hug your sister girls, we'll be back to St. Joe. before long to see her again."

The girls all hugged and walked back to Beverly's bed. Before climbing up, Beverly reached and grabbed Lynn and gave him a hug and a kiss. Lynn scrambled but not fast enough. Beverly laughed then climbed back into her bed. Nadine rolled the table with the dinner tray over in front of Beverly and Mary went to the foot of the bed to crank it up for her. Darlene laid some paper on the table beside the bed.

"I made you some paper dolls and doll clothes." She looked at Beverly. "I hope you like them."

"Thanks." Beverly said smiling.

"Bye Beverly," Betty said hugging her again.

"Bye Beverly," Mary said. "We'll be back soon."

Ralph gave the girls room to make their own farewells and then he went over and sat of the side of the bed. "Beverly, I think you'll be going home with the Doctor this week. I'll be coming down to see you on Wednesday at his house and bringing the rest of your clothes. Then we will make some plans for you to come home for a visit and for Betty to come to St. Joseph and spend some time with you here." Ralph leaned over to give his little girl a hug of his own then looked into Beverly's eyes. They were filled with tears.

"All right, Daddy."

Ralph got up and to no one in particular said, "Let's go." The girls waved and yelled good-byes as they walked from the ward toward the elevators. Once in the car and tired from an afternoon in a strange place, and feeling the stress of the emotional departure, each one again retreated into quiet thought. A disturbing stillness descended upon Ralph as guilt and sadness and a lack of confidence in his parenting fought to inhabit his mind. He looked over at his children. Lynn and Betty were both asleep and they had barely left the city behind. Ralph felt better as he drove through the country toward home. He knew this land like the back of his hand. He knew he was doing the best he could. His mind began to line up the day ahead. He liked to plan and set goals then work like the devil to accomplish them. Hard work was all he knew. It fed his spirit. As they approached the small town of Craig, Ralph called to Betty to wake up because they were almost to town and would be dropping her off at the Preston's house to spend the night. He pulled onto the main street and drove slowly up to the Preston's home. They did not live too far from Aunt Emma and Uncle Loren.

"We're here," Ralph said as he pulled up. He saw them in the back yard about the same time that they saw his car and they all came walking around to the front. Everyone climbed out of the car and Betty grabbed her sack of clothes.

"Hello," Ralph waved to Galen Preston, Ann's father, then reached out to shake his hand. Ralph pushed his hat back onto his head and nodded at Pauline, Ann's mother. She smiled. Ralph noticed for the first time that she was a pretty woman. He did not usually pay much attention to that kind of thing because his mind was too busy. But for now he leaned against his car glad to visit a moment, still trying to shake off the bad feelings he'd had. Finally, the sun began to set and shaking hands once again with Galen, Ralph said his goodbyes. Galen promised to get Betty home by suppertime Monday evening and Ralph left with only Mary, Darlene, Nadine and Lynn. It seemed the family he and Bessie had together was shrinking by the day. Ralph tuned north and headed home.

The country roads greeted them with the endless dirt and grit. Finally they saw their house, surrounded by the old outbuildings all framed by the setting sun. The swing hung in the still air as though frozen in time. Ralph pulled into the yard and shut off the motor. He saw Ralph Wendell assessing the small shed so he walked over to talk about the work they needed to do in the next few weeks. The girls went into the house, hopefully, Ralph was thinking, to start supper. They usually had pancakes on Sunday nights and then popped corn later while listening to the radio. Ralph looked forward to the evening and falling asleep in the old chair that he'd claimed over the years.

Ralph walked around the shed to check the materials he had and which ones he needed to pick up in town and made a mental note. Then he went towards the house where the aroma of food wafted out at him.

"Pancakes!" Mary called out. Ralph was surprised that Mary appeared to be in charge in the kitchen as he came in and hung up his hat. He sat down and took off his shoes and put them under his chair where he would not trip over them.

"Where's Nadine?" Ralph asked wondering if they were arguing again.

"She said I might as well learn how to cook pancakes." Mary said importantly, "Since she will be going to school soon, I told her I wanted to start doing the cooking."

Ralph figured that Mary was thinking that if she did the cooking, that would leave Darlene to do the dishes. He knew that Mary hated doing dishes.

"Here you go." She set a plate stacked with pancakes in front of him. They looked fine to him. Ralph smeared them with butter and poured maple syrup over them and began to eat. Lynn came in.

"Where's mine?" He whined. Lynn would need to go to bed early tonight..

"Here you go." Mary had a smaller stack on a plate and set it before Lynn. Ralph helped him put the butter and the syrup on them and cut them up. Nadine and Darlene strolled in.

Nadine looked at the pancakes and walked over to the cook-stove where Mary was working. "They look good, Mary."

"They are good." Ralph said giving support to Mary.

"Here, try some." Mary put some on a plate for Nadine and scooped up another one for Darlene.

"Thanks." The girls took their plates and sat down. Mary followed with a plate for herself..

"Nadine, did you get the paper work sent in for school?" Ralph asked.

"I put it in the mail last week. Dad, I need to buy a few things to take to school." Nadine proceeded to see if she could just get permission to make a purchase without having to give him the details of her list.

"What do you need?" Ralph would never understand why a girl needed so many more things than it took to raise a boy.

"Well I need some paper and pencils and then some personal items." Nadine pushed ahead with her request hoping that by emphasizing with the personal part, Dad would back off from the usual inquisition. Nadine did not want to discuss underwear with him even if it meant doing without.

"Did you check through that box of your Mother's things?" Ralph was not about to ask what the personal items were but he did not understand why Nadine could not wear Bessie's old personal items.

"Yes," said Nadine. "But they don't fit me." She was not about to discuss sizes of underwear with her father so left it at that.

"How much money do you need?"

"I'm not sure, but Aunt Ruth said she would take me with her shopping up to Shenandoah next Tuesday if you'd let me go." Aunt Ruth was special to all of them, but Nadine thought Aunt Ruth was the only one who really understood her.

"Tuesday?" Ralph thought about the week before him. Sunday would be over in a few hours and it would be back to the rush and push of work. "All right, Nadine." He thought she might as well get whatever it was she needed because it wouldn't be long before she would be gone and the other girls might as well get used to getting along without her.

Nadine got up and began to clear the dishes. Mary took the kettle of hot water from the stove and filled the wash bucket.

"Darlene, it's your turn to do the dishes." Nadine looked at her.

Ralph pushed back his chair and picked up Lynn. "Come on, son. You're getting ready for bed." Ralph carried Lynn out of the kitchen to his own bedroom where Lynn's little bed stood in the corner. All the children slept in that same bed until they were old enough to sleep upstairs on their own. Beverly moved up when she was five to be with her sisters. He did not know if Lynn would ever move upstairs. He and Ralph had become pals through-out the years after Bessie died. Ralph wasn't sure if he clung to Lynn or Lynn clung to him, but either way there seemed to be a cord that bound them together. He heard the girls in the kitchen as he helped Lynn get into the pajamas Aunt Ruth had sewn for him. He wished Lynn had a mother. He knew Lynn was well taken care of but young boys needed a Mother. Ralph knew his parenting skills were rough. One day he'd let Lynn get by with too much and the next he'd take a switch to him hard. A woman would balance things out. Yes, Ralph thought, he should consider getting married again. He thought about Elizabeth Yates coming over on Wednesday and smiled. Maybe he'd start courting her.

Chapter 5

Cindy and I crawled into the truck bed and found seats side by side between Cody and Jack. Unfortunately the man Cindy warned me about took the seat across from us. It was apparent he had not taken any opportunity to wash up and he still reeked of beer. In the freshness of the morning he did not seem as threatening, but he made me uncomfortable. I looked out at the driver who was checking the ropes of the tarp. He pulled the back gate down into place and jumped into his seat up front. Smoke from the rear end didn't fail to escort us out of the camp but sputtered out of the tail pipe loudly with popping noises. The old truck rattled and bumped across the uneven ground and down the road heading north. Cindy and I smiled at each other. Most of the men were settling into quiet chatter; a few had closed their eyes to nap. I assumed they had been part of the noise that went on all night. I was hoping the dirty cowboy would lean into his own space and fall asleep.

The sun was making its way up through the sky but in the moving truck the heat did not yet affect us. Cindy was telling us about the time she spent with her sister and the baby. It was obvious that Cindy was happy with life and looked forward to being in the family way. She said her sister had named her baby Robert Roy after his two grandfathers. It seemed a pretty big name for a baby, but I guessed he would grow into it.

"I think I'd like my first to be named after Cody." Cindy said dreamily. "Of course we wouldn't call him Cody because that would just be too confusing."

"What's Cody's full name?" I asked.

"Cody Evan," Cindy said. "Do you think Evan is a good name to call a boy?"

I thought about that. I had never in my life just sat around thinking up baby names. The whole idea of deciding a name before you ever saw the baby was a new one to me. I figured once you had the baby, you'd look at it and a name would come to you that just fit.

"I think Evan is a nice name." I finally said. "What if it's a girl?"

"Well," Cindy continued as much to herself as to me, "I thought that if I had a girl, I'd name her Sara Coreen after my Mother. What do you think of that name, Johnnie Belle?"

"That's pretty." I wondered if I would ever marry and have to face the task of naming a child. It was more than I wanted to think about right now. I looked over at Jack. He had his head back and appeared to be sleeping. Cody's body was leaning as well, with his eyes closed, and was either sleeping or wanting to remain out of this conversation.

I glanced in the direction of the man across from me. He was smiling in a sneering kind of way and was very much awake. His arms were folded across his chest. He tipped his hat forward and nodded at me. I looked down not acknowledging him at all. I looked at Cindy but she was lost in her dreams of motherhood. The man had a look of meanness about him. He was different than the others. For the most part, the men looked tired and seemed only concerned with working and getting back to their families. You could tell it from their talk about their wives and children and how they missed home.

"You girls ever do field work before?" The man leaned forward and directed himself right at me. His voice was husky, rough, and low. It made me shiver just to hear it, but quietly I nodded my head just slightly hoping to discourage further discourse.

At least Cindy noticed and she looked at me. I looked back at her. We were so close to the man that it was difficult to ignore anything, especially direct conversation. I wondered what he'd do if I straight out told him that I did not want to talk to him, but that would have taken a lot more nerve than I had. I wondered if my face reflected the fear I felt.

"Have you ever traveled with a work crew before?" He continued, ignoring my nod as a sign that I did not want to talk.

"No." I said speaking softly, but curtly then looked at Cindy for help.

"Johnnie Belle," she smiled at me. "We'd better catch a nap ourselves because this is going to be a long ride today."

I smiled at her tensely appreciating her suggestion and the help it was meant to be.

"You're right." I replied and leaned against the truck side. I felt Cindy move toward Cody and then we were both still. Closing my eyes I tried to rest, afraid if I looked the man would be staring back to call our bluff. I decided to really try to sleep because what Cindy said was true and because sleeping would help to pass the time.

As I relaxed with my eyes closed I thought about what I would write in a letter home. I would not talk about my apprehension, because Mama did not need one more worry on her. I would write about the tent being put up at the fair grounds for us to sleep under, the sounds of people playing cards and the music that drifted through the darkness. She'd probably liked to hear about the breakfast they had prepared for us, too. Mama would want to know that we were eating well. I would tell her about the man who gave me a paper to read and about Cindy and Cody and the friendship that had developed between us. That would make Mama happy. I would ask about Harold and tell him to help around the house. I wondered when we would get to the next town and if there would be a store that sold postcards or writing paper. I knew Jack had some money and though I wasn't sure how much it was, I figured he'd let me spend some for a letter home.

I sat up, my eyes opening to the dark man who sat across from me framed by the bright sunlight that was now streaming through the slats in the truck. Thrust back into the reality of my tiny space between Cindy and Jack, I yawned nervously and looked around to see if we were stopping at a town or merely a crossroads. I saw a few houses and then more and felt the truck swing into a turn. Looking around I saw stores and a huge building in the center of a square of streets. There was a park area around the building which appeared to have doors on every side.

"This is the county seat." Jack ventured. "That is the courthouse."

Everybody in the truck was looking beyond the panels, anxious to get out. The heat was beginning to take its toll on us and the odor of our close group was beginning to get a bit offensive. A break from the ride would be welcome indeed.

"What town is this?" Cody asked Jack.

"It's Independence." A man from the other side of the truck spoke up. Everyone was looking around and gathering up their things ready to be released from the cramped cell that held them. I threw a covert look at the man sitting across from me hoping he would get out first.

"Be seein' ya' later, sweetheart." He smiled and I saw what was left of his yellowed teeth. Then he grabbed his bag and swung around towards the rear of the truck waiting for it to stop.

I was shocked and speechless. Jack grabbed at the man's arm to gain his attention. The man paused looking at Jack's hand on his arm.

"Mister," Jack let his hand drop. "You'd better keep to yourself and just leave the girls alone."

"You don't look like nobody's mama to me." The man

egged Jack on.

"You heard what I said, mister." Jack spoke directly and I was proud of him for standing up to the man for me.

The truck lurched to a stop. Jack let go of the man as he jumped out and others began to follow. Our attention was diverted to jumping out of the confining space and moving into the shade of a large group of trees. The man walked away from the truck and towards what looked to be the downtown area. The four of us stood watching him.

"Let's go over there." Cody pointed to an old picnic table near the water spigot. Some were there filling up their jars and others had headed toward the outhouse. The man in charge was calling for everyone to come back to the truck so he could give us information about lunch. We were to get our lunch in the basement of a church a few blocks down the street. The Salvation Army was feeding crews who were passing through for a donation of a few cents each. After shaking the cramps from our legs, and refilling our jars, the four of us headed to the outhouse line.

One of the men from the truck stuck his hand out towards Jack.

"Howdy. The name's Cooper. Audie Cooper." His accent was southern but he didn't sound like he was from Arkansas.

"Jack. Jack Veazey." Jack shook hands with him.

"That feller's a bad'n. Name's Dirk. I trucked up with him last year an' he's a roughun' that'n is. You'n don't wanna be gittin in it with him." Audie Cooper shook his head and looked up at the sky as if to catch the breeze and he wiped the sweat from the back of his neck on a dirty handkerchief pulled from his pocket.

"I don't want to be getting into it with anybody." Jack said. "But I ain't a gonna stand there and have a man act that-a-way with my sister."

"Look-e-here," Audie Cooper went on. "I don,t a-care bout nothin', but I know'd he can whup a young pup the likes a you'n with one hand. I's a jist a-tellin' ya' to watch yer back."

Jack looked at the man and knew he was just trying to warn him. "Thanks." Jack said. "I will. Where you from?"

"Oklahoma ways. It's worser there. Most my folks headed west as they lost their farms, but I came to Arkansas with my wife's family and I still cain't seem to make any money to count."

Audie Cooper said no more as we took turns using the outhouse and our little group broke away from the others.

We gathered again near the picnic table and then walked in the direction that the others had gone. Our stomachs ached for the food that we hoped would be good, filling and not cost too much. None of us spoke as we took in the lay of the town. We approached the big square shopping area that surrounded the courthouse. It was busy with town's people visiting on the sidewalks, probably taking a break from the stifling heat in the stores. We walked by a fabric store with prints that looked like gardens filled with flowers and beautiful sewing baskets. There were some offices and businesses, a dentist sign hung at the bottom of a staircase next to a drugstore with a soda fountain. All four of us moved slowly past the big window at the front of the drugstore gazing at a group of young people eating large dishes of ice cream at the bar.

"Oh, there's a dime store, Jack. Let's run in and I'll get some notepaper to write Mama a letter." I walked up to the door that was between two windows filled with knick-knacks. "It won't take a minute." I knew everyone could barely think from hunger.

Cindy, Cody, and Jack followed me into the shop and I asked the woman at the counter where the notepaper was. As

I followed her down a narrow aisle she asked if we were from out of town. I knew our southern accent would give us away more and more as we traveled north.

"Yes." I replied then picked up a small package and a pencil and walked back to the counter where the cash register was sitting.

"How much are these?" I asked trying to sound more like a woman than I was.

"That's fifteen cents." The woman rang up the purchase and Jack paid.

Walking outside after making my purchase, I felt different. I felt more grown up. Maybe it was making decisions on my own and learning to deal with things without Mama. Whatever it was, I decided that I liked it.

At the next corner we waited for an old wagon pulled by mules to go by and then crossed the hard packed dirt street. Dust seemed to be everywhere we went. I was about as dirty as I'd ever been in my life and wondered when I'd get a real bath in a tub of hot water. The church steeple rose up behind the grocery store that was across the street. We headed that way and saw some of the men from our truck in a line going into a side door. We walked across a parking area and into the door as the line moved toward the smell of food.

"I smell cornbread." Cody said with a smile.

"When we settle down, I'm going to bake cornbread and cobblers and raise chickens." Cindy said.

I smiled. Cindy's ideas and dreams were sparking the same in my own mind. I saw myself at a stove baking cornbread with a handsome man washing his hands at the sink. I might even want to have a baby too.

"Now, that sounds good to me." Jack said. "You sure knew what you were doing when you got Cindy to marry you, Cody."

Cody put his arm around Cindy and gave her a hug. "You don't have to tell me something I already know."

The line finally got up to the kitchen where two women were serving up beans and cornbread. We each took our own with polite thanks.

The boys followed Cindy and me to a table near an open window and sat down. We ate in silence each of us feeling liberated by the open spaces, fresh air, and good food.

After eating all we could hold, we pushed back from the table feeling full.

Jack just patted his stomach.

"I think we'd better go walk this off if we are going to face an afternoon riding in that truck again." Cody looked at Cindy to see if she agreed.

"I'd really like to stretch out on the ground and relax, but you're right about needing to walk. What about you Johnnie Belle?" Cindy looked at me.

"I'd like to walk, too,." I said getting up to clear our dishes.

"Me too," Jack pushed his chair back and helped me.

We strolled up a sidewalk and walked away from the shopping area. We headed down a street with houses neatly lined up on either side. A few of the streets had brick on them. There were lots of trees for shade and the day felt good. We circled back around until we came up on the far side of the park where the truck was. Contented, with full stomachs and a walk, the close quarters of the truck did not seem quite as terrible as it had before. If we worked it right, I thought, we might be able to avoid being in close proximity with that nasty Dirk.

I watched as Cindy, Cody, and Jack climbed on top of the picnic table and sat down. I decided to walk to the outhouse alone since it was within sight. Cindy leaned on

Cody and he put his arm around her.

"I'll be right back." I told them and walked across the park. I thought that having a husband like Cody, who could give a girl such loving protection, might be something I'd like. I'm already a changed girl, I decided. Thinking about men, marriage, and children was certainly novel for me.

I held my breath as long as I could but came out of the privy gasping for fresh air. Looking down the street I saw our truck driver open the hood of the truck again. He was putting in more water and maybe some oil or something. I wasn't sure what he was checking for but it made me feel secure that he was keeping an eye on possible trouble. As I walked back in that direction, I saw Jack walk over to look into the engine. Always acting like he knew more than he did.

In some ways, it seemed like we'd been on the road more than two days. Being cooped up with the same people for long periods makes you really become a part of them whether you liked it or not. I knew I had never let myself get this close to kids at school, but then desks at school sat at least a foot apart and you were always busy with your own work. Most of the time kids left other kids alone except when they decided to pick on somebody or tease someone younger or smaller. I remembered Sister being teased because she couldn't hear well and didn't always pronounce her words right. Arriving near the table where Cindy and Cody had stretched out together on the cool grass, I took a drink of water from my jar, screwed the lid back on tight, then sprawled out as well. Thinking back I realized that I never made any real effort to try to become friends with other kids because it would betray Sister. It had not occurred to me that some of the kids at school might be nice. I laughed thinking I might actually have enjoyed getting close to one or two of the girls in my class. Well, I'd never know now. Funny how looking back lets you see things so differently.

Life is a good teacher, but sometimes you've got to

rummage through the experience before you recognize the lesson. Maybe going off, away from family, is what gives a person time to wonder and think about these kinds of things. I wonder if Mama knew that I'd be learning things just riding on this truck. Experience. That's what Mama called it. Mama talked about experience all the time. Now I know some of what she was talking about. I wondered what other experiences I was about to step into? I got up, refilled my water and looked at the men who were gathering around the truck.

"Load up!" The driver yelled and everybody shuffled slowly toward the truck. No one was in any hurry to be sandwiched back inside. Jack came around, grabbed his stuff and stood patiently beside Cody. When it was our turn, we threw our bags in and climbed up. I took a seat that had room for only two others right next to it, but was surrounded by men that did not look particularly unfriendly. Cindy and Cody took the seats by me and Jack sat near but not against us. I had hoped nasty Dirk might get left, but he showed up at last, climbed in, and took a seat at the very rear helping to pull down the gate that held us all in. The driver climbed up on the side and said we'd break again in the late afternoon to eat, then go on to Shenandoah arriving late.

I looked at Cindy and then over at Jack and Cody. It would be a long afternoon. But I was feeling surer of myself. Taking out the paper I had purchased, I put the box, emptied of Mama's cookies, on my lap and began to write.

It didn't take long before I had several pages filled.

"What all are you writing, Johnnie Belle?" Jack asked.

"Do you want to read it?" I asked him, because I did not want to repeat the whole letter to him, nor did I want to read my personal letter aloud so everyone on the truck could hear it.

"Sure," Jack seemed surprised that I would make such

an offer. I handed him the letter and crammed the cookie box back into the food sack that was under my seat.

Jack read the letter slowly. He'd never been a good reader and it would take him awhile. I waited patiently, though I was ready to take a nap again. After two days on this truck, I wondered how we'd stand up to a day in the fields. Finally Jack handed the letter back and I put it into the envelope that I'd already addressed and slipped it into my pocket. I felt like I'd had a conversation with Mama and happiness seeped through me. I patted my pocket as if protecting the small package that was ready to mail at the next stop. Jack leaned back, his arms folded. I made a pillow on my lap with my bag and put my head down. It was hot. Even the breeze was hot. But the rocking of the truck and the noise of the tires on the road lulled me off to Star City where Mama and Harold were sitting at the table reading my letter.

In my dream, I tried to call out to Mama but she didn't hear me. She just kept reading my letter with tears in her eyes and telling Harold everything I said. Mr. Jim was on the divan snoring. He was wearing a dirty brown cowboy hat. I was afraid to look at him. Harold was eating cookies and there, on the shelf where Mama kept family pictures, was a picture of Cindy and Cody with their laps full of children.

"Johnnie Belle," Jack was nudging my shoulder. "We're coming into a town and I think we may be stopping. At least I hope we are. I need a break."

"What?" I woke up feeling a little sick from eating too much cornbread, or more likely from being in the back of a hot truck for too long.

"I said I think we're stopping for a break." Jack repeated himself.

Just then the truck pulled up and stopped. It was another small town with a scrubby looking park. Men were slowly jumping out of the truck appearing wearier than before lunch, probably from the heat. I rose slowly unsure if my stomach would stay put and breathed the fresh air that filled the truck now that most of the men had cleared out of the way.

When it was our turn to jump down, Jack went first and reached up to help me. Cindy and Cody sauntered up a hill to the outhouse where, once again, a line had formed. Jack must have sensed that the heat had gotten the best of me as he walked slower than normal. He handed me his jar of water and told me to drink some. We stopped for a moment under the shade of a tree while I drank. I began to feel better. Jack drank then and screwed the lid back on. We walked on toward the line smelling the horrible odor emanating from the one and only outhouse. I knew it was made worse by the heat of the day. Flies buzzed around us as we waited silently, too numb from the hot trip to think.

I remembered my letter.

"Jack, do we have time to mail my letter here?" I asked him.

One of the men heard me and turned around to look at my letter. I knew he'd seen me writing it and he smiled.

"I think we'll be here for about half an hour," he said and nodded at me. "The truck is overheatin' and they gonna hav' ta let her cool."

"Thank you." I said.

Jack once again stuck out his hand to introduce himself as the line gradually moved closer to the buzzing of the flies and the smell.

"I'm Jack Veazey and this is my sister, Johnnie Belle." Jack nodded toward me.

"I'm Vince Maynard from south of Star City. Where you folks from?"

"We are from Star City. Born and raised there." Jack was trying to sound older than he was, but I just smiled.

"Ya' goin to Shenandoah or further north?" Vance Maynard asked us.

"We're going to try the outfit at Shenandoah." Jack said. Heard they got some bunks fit for women there and we aim to earn us some money. Nothing growing back home."

"Me too," The man replied. "Got six kids back home and got to feed 'em."

Cindy was just coming out and Cody was going in. Cindy came back to where we were.

"Hi." She seemed as tired as I felt. Sweat was running down her face. I'm going to go lay down on the blanket. I feel a little sick."

"So do I." I confessed. "We'll be there, by and by."

Cody came out and whacked Jack on the back. We watched the two of them walk towards the place where they had put their blanket, shake it out onto the dry ground and lay down. Then we turned our weary bodies back to the line and waited some more.

Finally it was my turn. It was worse than I had imagined. I got out as quickly as I could manage. I did not even wait to speak to Jack as he went in. I just ran across the park towards the place Cindy and Cody lay across the blanket on the dry grass.

"Here, you can share the blanket." Cindy said rolling over to give me room.

"Thanks, but I think the ground is cooler." I had found a small patch of grass, dry and scratchy, but surely not as hot as a blanket.

"How do you feel now?" Cindy asked.

"Better, I think." I gazed up at the blue sky, breathing in the sweet air. "I was feeling pretty sick. I guess I ate too much dinner."

"Me too," Cindy giggled.

Then I giggled and it felt so good. I felt free. Hot, sweaty, but free. This was already a real adventure for me. I was really glad for the first time that I had gotten on that truck and rolled on with my life. Not that I did not miss Mama and Harold, but I would see them again. Meanwhile, life was happening to me.

Jack flopped on the grass beside me.

"Let's lay here a few minutes. Then we'll walk down the road and see if there is a place to post your letter."

"Ok." I said breathing slowly and trying to lose the feeling of movement that hours in the truck had patterned in my brain. We all lay there just enjoying the freshness of the air when Cindy jumped up.

"I feel like running," she cried. "Come on you guys, let's run up the street."

I jumped up and knew that the short rest was all we needed and that exercise was indeed in order and would even feel mighty good.

"Let's go!" I said.

The boys looked at each other, jumped up and raced past us. Cindy and I followed but not nearly as fast. We were laughing and galloping as hard as we could.

"Oh." I gasped as we caught up to the boys. They stood in the shade of an awning that gripped the front of a building over a store window.

"That felt great." Cindy smiled as she panted.

"Let's go in here since it looks to be the only store this town has." Jack suggested.

Jack held the door for Cindy and me, and we entered. It was small and dark and had everything one could imagine stacked nearly to the ceiling. I couldn't help but look everywhere all at once. It was actually amazing that any one store could sell so many things.

"Can we post a letter here?" I heard Jack ask the clerk.

"Sure can." The little man said. "Where you from? Down south?"

"Yes sir." Jack replied. "We're on our way to Shenandoah to work in the fields."

"I hear the farmin' up there is good this summer." The man went on.

"We hope so." Jack said as I gave the man the letter. He looked at the address then at me.

"You two look too young to be married." He said questioningly.

"We're not." I jumped in disgusted at the thought. "We're brother and sister."

"We're married." Cindy said smiling and grabbing Cody's arm.

"Well, I'll be." The man said smiling. "They just get younger ever' day."

We all laughed and thanked the man and left. Outside, Cody and Cindy linked arms and headed back towards the park.

"I guess that's all there is to this town." Jack said and we followed the two newlyweds back towards the truck and the final leg of the trip.

"You know, Jack." I began. "I am glad I came."

"I knew you would be eventually." Jack said to me.

"I think I'm going to like being on my on and grown up." I told Jack. "At home I always felt like Mama's little girl. Out here I feel like Johnnie Belle Veazey, becoming a woman." I laughed.

"You are." Jack said seriously. "It's hard to grow up when everyone around you sees you as a kid. You never really think for yourself and thinking for yourself is the only way to really learn about yourself and life."

I got the feeling Jack was musing about his own life more than mine. I rarely heard him talk so seriously.

"You know Jack, I never looked at you like you were really a grown man. I've always seen you as a bothersome brother." I laughed smiling with recognition that Jack indeed had grown up. "Life is certainly amazing isn't it Jack?" I looked again at Jack as we neared the truck.

"Amazing." Jack said looking back at me. Our eyes met with a kind of new recognition about each other.

We rejoined the group, climbed reluctantly back into the truck and found our seats. I watched Dirk come across the road toward the truck. I wondered why he always took off in a different direction than the rest of us. I wondered what he did. He was again the last to get on and he helped shut the gate again.

Everyone was talking, relieved with the break and knowing that the trip was near an end. A breeze was starting to blow and a few clouds had surfaced to cover the sun. It was an encouraging sign of rain and made everyone feel excited. Talk was louder than it had been yet. I guess, too, that by now there were a lot more acquaintances than before, maybe a sense of camaraderie. Everyone was more open. One man began to talk about the place in Shenandoah and his experiences from last year. He talked about the out buildings and how they'd made an old chicken house into a bunk house for men and an old storage shed that was nearer the house into a place for the women folk. I perked up to listen. He told about the shower house they had for the men out doors, but they had a big tub for the women inside their quarters.

Cindy and I looked at each other and smiled. Then I

frowned.

"Cindy," I said. "You won't be able to stay with Cody."

"No." Cindy said sadly. "But I knew that. We decided that until we earn enough to get on our own, we could stand to be separated. It will just make us work harder."

I was impressed with Cindy and Cody more at that moment than I had been the whole trip, seeing their willingness to sacrifice and work hard. I hoped some day I might share my life with a man too, and we could work hard together towards the future.

The man who had made this trip last year was talking about the fields and the black dirt they had in this part of Missouri as well as further north in Iowa. He said the dirt was as black as coal and the rivers kept it moist for growing most anything. We could hardly believe that the drought that had permeated the whole country the last few years had left anyplace with wet fields, but it sure sounded good. I thought about the cotton fields and how year after year they had gotten dryer and dryer until nothing had come up this year at all. Mama said she'd never seen it that bad before. I wondered if this man knew what he talked about. The dust storms had probably reeled through Iowa like Oklahoma and Kansas. We might all be disappointed. If there wasn't any work, I didn't know how Jack and I would live, but I might as well not worry about that now.

"I think they ought to put the women in the same bunkhouses as the men." Everyone got quiet and stared toward the man called Dirk who had taken off his dirty old hat. It was plain enough now to see where he had gone off to at our last stop. He was drinking from a bottle that was wrapped up in a sack. Drinking was the biggest evil I knew about. I looked at Cindy and then at Jack, scared to be so close to a mean and drunk man.

"Dirk, why don't you jist shut up afore you git yurself in trouble." Audie Cooper gave him a warning look.

"Why that cute little thing would be just right to snuggle up to at night." The dark man looked right at me.

Jack jumped up and lunged at the man. Two other men grabbed him. Jack had his fists up, and was trying to pull away and go after the drunk.

"I'll teach you how to talk around a woman." Jack yelled.

I sat stunned and embarrassed. Sure that red color was creeping up my neck and across my face, I looked down.

Another worker stood up, grabbed the man's bottle and hurled it out of the truck. Then he pointed his finger into the face of the dark man. "You start this drinkin' again and you are off this truck for good! You hear? We put up with you last time and we won't do it again."

The dark man leaned in a corner sulking and quiet. Several of the men shook their heads at him and looked helplessly at Jack. Jack looked angry and ready to kill. I had seen Jack get mad before. He was so angry he couldn't talk. I knew he would not normally be put off so easily. He was probably just saving his anger to be dispelled at a later time. Jack never backed down easily. It certainly put a damper on the group. Everybody settled back into their own little hole and a man someone had called Max got out his harmonica and began to play. It soothed the nerves of everyone on the truck. Even I felt somewhat calmer though still anxious. I finally looked around and saw that no one was staring at me anymore. I looked at Cindy and she looked scared too.

"I don't feel safe with him around." She whispered.

"Neither do I." I agreed.

We didn't say more but I'm sure we were both thinking about how we'd handle a situation if it arose. I wondered how this experience would look when time had passed. I'd seen some drunken men, and I knew they could be dangerous. I'd never had to personally deal with one and I hoped that this would be it. Cody was patting Jack on the back. I knew that Jack was festering inside. His anger would surface again before too much longer and Dirk had better be ready.

Daylight turned to dusk and the farms just kept rolling by. I couldn't tell by looking if the crops were any good or not. I didn't see any cotton that's for sure. Working in the fields would be a relief after riding in this truck. Leaning back once more, I was unsure if I wanted to sleep or not. Feeling anxious about the first night at our destination, and wondering about all the future and what it held, I grasped once more for my memories of Mama and Star City.

Chapter 6

Ralph felt tired, dirty and hungry. Pushing his hat back and wiping his forehead, he headed for home. Glad to be rid of the load of pigs that he'd hauled for Smith, he enjoyed the rush of the wind through the open window. The sun was just meeting the tree line and streaks of orange began to smear across the horizon. Ralph was wondering what was for supper when he remembered it was Wednesday and Elizabeth Yates was bringing their dinner. Maybe he was taking advantage of Elizabeth. Since he was alone with his children now, and she had been alone for some time, he sensed marriage was in her plans somewhere down the road. He did like the attention she gave him but there just wasn't any spark with Elizabeth. Maybe he was too old to be courting again. Maybe he should just give in and marry her so the children would have a mother. She was nice enough and she liked his family. They'd known each other since they were kids.

He sighed and watched the sun setting in the sky. Right now he was just tired and dirty and wanted to get home. He had forgotten to tell the girls she was coming, but if they got something cooked before Elizabeth got there they could put it in the icebox and hold it a day. He hoped Ralph Wendell had gotten more ice today and picked up those supplies for the shed. Right now he had too much on his mind to be thinking about a woman.

Ralph swung his truck off the main road and back-tracked north a ways. All he could think about was dinner. Seeing the house, ahead he honked the horn, a habit he had developed when he'd left Lynn at home with the girls. Lynn would run out of the house on stubby little legs, browned from both sun and dirt, and Ralph would reach for him, swinging him up into the branches of the tree. He loved that little boy.

He saw the Yates's car in the yard. It was hard to get used to. Matthew Yates had been dead for years, but Ralph still thought of Elizabeth and him as a couple. Maybe that's why he couldn't seem to muster romantic feelings for her. His stomach rumbled and he realized that, for now, all he could think about was supper.

Lynn came running from the house as usual and came up just as Ralph swung open the heavy truck door. He greeted him with a playful swat across the back side and then placed his dirty old straw had on Lynn's head. Lynn pushed it back off his forehead, turned and raced towards the back door, not waiting for his dad today. He went in tossing the hat onto a chair. Following Lynn through the porch, Ralph picked up the hat and hung it on the old nail that had been pounded there years ago. He sat down, pulled off his boots, and left them on the porch, since they had company, and then went into the kitchen. Elizabeth was there setting the table. A big plate of ham was sliced and a skillet of potatoes had been fried up. She'd cooked corn on the cob, green beans, and sliced up some big tomatoes. Elizabeth had a garden and canned enough food every year for a whole town. His own gardening was small since he was gone trucking so much. The girls were not very good at keeping it growing. It was a sore spot with him.

"Hello, Ralph." Elizabeth smiled and looked up. She looked so fresh and clean compared to how he felt. He knew he smelled like the hogs he had trucked. He went directly to the wash stand and began to apply the lye soap the girls learned to make from helping their mother. . He used to be more careful about his looks, but he was too busy anymore to give it too much time. He thought about what he looked like in his courting days when he'd get spiffed up to go see Bessie. He'd put on clean clothes and slick back his shiny black hair. Somehow he wasn't feeling the spark that lit those fires anymore. He glanced in the mirror and combed his hair down some then walked over to the table.

"Well, this looks just fine, Elizabeth. Did the girls all run off and leave you?" Ralph heard them at the piano singing and playing, unusual for this time of day.

"I told them if they would serenade me, I would do the kitchen duties." Elizabeth smiled prettily. Ralph was sure the girls were glad to take her up on that offer.

Ralph wasn't too much with gushy words, but he smiled and nodded as he went into the living room to listen to the girls. He sat down in his chair and noticed that Lynn had rejoined Elizabeth's two boys on the floor rolling on top of each other. They looked more like pups than boys. Ralph enjoyed watching them, listening to the girls sing and hearing Elizabeth hum in the kitchen. There was a peace about it.

"Dinner's ready." Elizabeth announced as she came into the living room.

"OK, let's all get washed up." Ralph clapped his hands together and ushered everyone into the kitchen where they took turns washing at the basin then moved to find seats around the big oak table. It was almost strange to see it filled up again. He walked over to the table and sat down. Elizabeth handed him the potatoes, and touching his shoulder, sat down beside him.

Dinner was delicious and Ralph felt satisfied and happy. They all went out on the front porch after the last of the pie was gone and watched the boys catch lightening bugs. Ralph told Lynn to go get his harmonica off the dresser. It had been a long time since he'd taken the time to play. Lynn came running back out and handed the instrument to Ralph, then ran on out in the yard. Ralph blew the cobwebs out and softly began to play. Everything reminded him of a happier day. The melody was soulful and low. Ralph was too tired for any barn dance tune. The night was still and the bullfrogs from Smith's pond sounded like they were in an uproar over something.

"Elizabeth, this is nice." Ralph said.

"I've enjoyed the evening too." Elizabeth reached out and touched Ralph's arm. "But I must get the boys home to bed now."

Ralph rose off the step where he'd found a post to lean on and took Elizabeth's hand, helping her up as well. It was more of a gentlemanly gesture than a romantic one.

"Boys," she called. "Let's go."

"How's your car running?" Ralph asked, not that he could work on a car, but he knew she'd had some trouble with it last month.

"Fine," Elizabeth said smiling at his practicality.

They walked to her car and Ralph opened the front door. The boys both tumbled into the front seat and Elizabeth climbed in after them. Ralph slammed the door shut and stood back.

Elizabeth looked up at him.

"I hope we can do this more often." She said.

Ralph smiled and she started the car still looking up at him. Ralph watched her drive off into the night. He stood there in the silence wondering what life would be like to marry again and specifically what would it be like if he married Elizabeth. He thought about dinner and knew he would eat well.

"Daddy." Lynn yelled. "Look at all the lightening bugs I caught."

Ralph pulled himself back to the present and walked slowly toward the light coming from the front of the house. Lynn met him and they walked together into the house to get ready for bed. He didn't see the girls and assumed they were upstairs.

"Time to get to bed," Ralph told Lynn.

It did not have to be said more than once tonight and Lynn headed that way.

"Wash up first." Ralph yelled to him.

Lynn came back from the bedroom to the kitchen and washed his hands and face then headed to bed. Ralph followed him into their room to see him to bed.

"Goodnight big boy." Ralph patted his behind and smiled as Lynn rolled over and probably fell right to sleep.

Ralph went back to his chair and turned on the radio to try and catch the last of the baseball game. Other than work and the children, baseball was his one passion in life. He closed his eyes and listened to the announcer until his own snoring woke him. The game was over and static was the only sound from the radio. He pulled his aching body out of the chair, turned off the radio set and made his way to bed. He could still hear the girls upstairs talking, but he was too tired to yell up at them. Besides, with Nadine about off to school, they needed some time to talk.

Ralph fell asleep wondering if it was okay to marry a woman because he liked her cooking. He supposed it'd been done. He dreamed about a table laden with ham, potatoes, and pie.

Ralph's life was a simple one, yet working and keeping the family going from one day to the next was at times a monumental task. His pleasures came from the small moments. Nadine's excitement as she prepared to move in with Mrs. Baxter and attend school, watching Betty and Beverly get back together for an afternoon of play and seeing Mary and Darlene begin to take over the household chores. Of course there were Lynn's little onerous ways that kept the entire family on their toes. Ralph Wendell was rarely home, but their relationship was a typical one that develops between a father and his first born son. They had an understanding between them that could not be explained. In some ways they were a lot alike.

Ralph constantly planned for the future. One day Lynn would begin school, and Ralph would not be able to take him on the road so much. He decided he'd purchase a few acres of land down the road and prepare it for planting. The bank approached him with it. If he had a good crop, it would practically pay for the land in a few years. Right now land was difficult to work and even harder to sell. It was a bargain and Ralph had confidence he could make it work. He was good at farming and Ralph seemed a natural at making land deals. He'd done it before and the bank trusted him. He knew the land and understood the worth of it. Besides that, there was a thrill in the art of making a good deal.

It had been a typically hot August and today Ralph was up on a board that was balanced between two saw horses. With a bucket of white paint in one hand and a big brush in the other, he was getting more paint on him than on the shed. He stopped to wipe his forehead with his arm when Mary came from the house with a big glass of water.

"Drink Daddy?" Mary asked.

He climbed down from his perch, and pushed back his hat.

"Thanks, Mary." He drank the water slowly. "I could probably use another one of those."

He watched her walk back toward the house thinking how much like her Mother she was. Painting in the heat of the sun was tiring. The sweat rolled down his back and face feeding salty drops into his mouth. He'd been worrying the idea of getting married again. Emma wouldn't let it alone. Even Ruth seemed to think it was necessary, and each of them had their own ideas as to who he should court. Maybe if he hired a man to help out with the work on the new land he'd purchased, he'd be able to give more time to finding a wife. Maybe if he wasn't so tired he could get more excited about one of the women he knew. The girls didn't seem to really take to any of them.

"Dad!" Mary yelled.

"What!" Ralph yelled back.

"We need more ice! Can we go into town today?" Mary was hanging on the screen door.

"Mary don't hang on that door. I just fixed it."

"Can we go into town?" Mary continued yelling.

"I need to finish this painting today." Ralph hollered back.

"Can Darlene and I drive into town and get it?" Mary asked sweetly.

Ralph understood now. Mary knew he would not stop painting until either the day or the job ended. He looked at her thinking about the short drive he'd taken down the road with them the day before.

"Where's Nadine?" he asked.

"She's ironing." Mary came running out to the shed, bringing another glass of water.

"So you and Darlene want to drive the car into town together, without Nadine, to get ice." Ralph repeated the plan that had surfaced quicker than butter could melt on a hot tin roof in July weather.

"Well, we could use the practice." Mary waited knowing that she was pretty good at talking their father into most anything. Darlene didn't use the same tactics. She'd ask, get an answer, and just accept it. Mary wheedled. Ralph considered. Well, what could it hurt? They sure needed the practice. And it would be better for all of them if he was not in the car. He looked at Mary.

"The keys are in it." He said simply.

Mary ran back to the house yelling at Darlene. Ralph smiled and turned back to painting. He hoped they'd keep the car on the road. He couldn't afford to be replacing tires right now. He looked up and saw the girls heading toward the big old black car.

"Mary." He called to them.

"What?" Mary asked.

"Who's doing the driving?"

"I'm driving there and Darlene's driving back." She answered.

"Well, be careful and don't forget the ice. Put it on the bill." Ralph went back, once more, to his painting and thought about when he learned to drive. He liked to drive. He took a drink of the water and it occurred to him that the water was all a part of the girls' plan. They were smart, those girls. He wondered if they'd be back in time to get dinner or if they'd talked Nadine into doing that tonight? Well, Nadine could hold her own with those two, he thought, as he kept his arm moving from one stroke into the next. There was little time in his life to stand still.

As the summer sun dropped into the western sky Ralph finished his work and stood back to look at the shed. Not a man with much patience for the details, Ralph thought it looked good enough. Cleaning up, he began to plan the trip he had to make up to Clarinda to truck a load of sweet corn. He would be bringing back a load of pigs to the St. Joe. stock yards. Next week he'd have to load up Nadine and her things to go to Chillicothe to Mrs. Baxter's.

Ralph lived like he worked, moving from task to task, keeping his eye down the road, avoiding emotional complication.

As Ralph washed up at the pump in the yard he saw the dust of an automobile coming up the road. He watched it until he saw it was the girls, then moved toward the garden to do some weeding. He remembered when he was a young man and caused his own share of trouble, and smiled as he watched the girls lug the block of ice into the house. Ralph picked a few onions and tomatoes, carried them back to the pump to wash them off and then eat them. There was nothing he loved better than fresh tomatoes from the garden with an onion or two. The summer seemed to be sucking the life out of everything and he yearned for fall, cooler air, and maybe rain.

Looking up, the dust from the road was rising again and floating as someone traveled from the south. Now he could see it was Smith with his team of horses hitched to his wagon. He waved. Ralph could see he'd been into town for his monthly shopping trip for supplies and was heading home. Ralph smelled beans cooking and something else. Going into the house he stripped off his old paint clothes and pulled on a somewhat cleaner set of work clothes that he kept hanging on the porch for that purpose. It was another habit he'd gotten from living with Bessie for so many years. She did not like dirt in her house. Ralph walked into the kitchen and found Nadine making a cake. They did not have cake often because sugar was too costly but Nadine could stretch a few pounds a long way.

"Cake tonight Nadine?" Ralph asked as he sat down to pull off his boots.

"It's Aunt Ruth's recipe." Nadine replied.

"Well, you can't do better than to cook like Aunt Ruth." Ralph went into the living room and sat down. The heat had tired him out more than he'd realized and he tuned his radio until he found a music show. Putting his feet up he watched Lynn and Betty through the front window. They were up in the tree. Darlene and Mary came bounding down the stairs and went into the kitchen to help Nadine with supper. Mary came back into the living room and sat down. He was glad his girls enjoyed music as much as he did. He figured that music could take you from wherever you were to anywhere you wanted to go without moving at all. There wasn't much in life that touched his soul more than music. Barn dancing music, church music, and radio music all had a way of transporting him somewhere away from the daily grind where work did not exist.

"Supper's ready." Nadine called.

Ralph and Mary jumped up.

"Go call the babies." Ralph told Mary. He always called the younger ones babies. Mary thought it was embarrassing sometimes when they were out at church or in town and Ralph would talk about his babies. Sometimes it was as if life stopped when Bessie died and the little ones remained forever in his mind as the babies.

Betty and Lynn tumbled through the house and went to the kitchen.

"It's hot in here." Betty complained.

"Wash your face and arms." Mary told her.

Betty did as she was told and rubbed the wet rag over her long skinny legs as well. Lynn picked up on this tactic and began to scrub himself as well. A muddy puddle evolved on the floor.

"You two put that rag down." Nadine told them disgusted at the mess she figured she would have to clean up.

"Now just look at the mess they've made." She went on. She mopped up the puddle and swatted Lynn on the backside.

"I didn't do it." Lynn yelled.

"You did too." Betty started in.

"Sit down." Darlene told them and she gave Lynn a stare that would churn the milk in a cow.

"That's enough." Ralph told them all before the whole

table erupted into a squabble and dinner got cold. Besides, he was hungry and wanted some of Nadine's cake.

"Did you girls have any trouble driving the old car?" Ralph asked them.

"No." Mary answered.

"No." Darlene echoed.

Ralph looked at them but decided not to pursue the conversation. Some things were better left alone. He remembered that from his own youth.

"Nadine, a week from Thursday we'll pack up your things and take you over to Mrs. Baxter's. Monday I have to truck sweet-corn up to Clarinda. Darlene, I need you and Mary to help me with the Smith's team of horses on Friday to clear a pasture I'm going to plant." Ralph seldom asked the girls to do farm work but he knew they could help drive the horses and he and Ralph Wendell could get the work done faster. It was going to be a big job to get it cleared before winter with everything else he'd scheduled.

"Why can't Ralph Wendell do that?" Mary asked reaching for the tomatoes. She did not like to do field work.

"He'll be there too, but I need extra help. It's been let go a long time."

"Daddy, can I go with you to clear the pasture?" Lynn looked up.

"Sure." Ralph said. "We can all go over there." Nadine you can bring lunch about noon that day. Betty can stay and help you."

"I can do that." Nadine said. She got up and cut the cake into squares. Bessie's old baking pans were still doing their job. They all dug in and there was little left. Ralph pushed his chair back, scraping it across the floor and patted his stomach. Though he didn't much care what he ate, he did love to eat and was partial to sweets.

"Nadine that was as good as Aunt Ruth herself could do." Ralph never pretended to know how easy or complicated cooking was but he was appreciative of all efforts his girls made in that area.

"Thank you, Daddy." She got up and began to clear the dishes.

"You other girls need to clean up in here and let Nadine do something else." Ralph said in his no nonsense voice that communicated there'd be no wheedling out of it and no use even trying. Mary and Darlene looked at each other and scowled.

"Doesn't Betty have to help?" Darlene suggested.

"Betty, you help your sisters tonight." Ralph looked at her.

"Lynn, you get the tub out and I'll pump you some water to get a bath."

"No!" Lynn screamed and ran through the living room and out the front door.

Ralph ignored him and went ahead with the bath preparations. When he was ready he called to Lynn. When Lynn did not come, Ralph went to the front door.

"Lynn, you can come now or I can get a switch off the tree and you can come then." He was tired and wanted to clean up and get ready for bed himself.

Lynn dropped from the tree and put his hands in his pockets and walked into the house scowling. Ralph swatted his backside lightly as Lynn hunched over, his overall straps hanging off his bony shoulders, and sobbed through the door frame and into the kitchen.

"It's not Saturday." Lynn wiped his eyes making his face muddy.

"No but you're more than dirty. Where did you go

today?" Ralph helped him to strip down and got him into the tub of water.

"Me and Betty played down by the road in that ditch." He said and yawned.

"No wonder you're filthy. Now wash up and I'll help you dry off."

Before long Ralph had Lynn into bed and he told Betty to follow in the tub. She did and then went upstairs where the other girls had gathered.

Ralph was weary. His muscles ached from a full day of the up and down motion of painting. His brain ached trying to keep up with his many responsibilities. His soul ached for someone to share his life. His children had been a comfort when Bessie passed, but it had been long enough now and he was starting to feel alone in the world. Maybe it was the fact that the girls were growing up and needed him less and less. With Beverly living with Doc. Miller, the needs of his family were changing and his own needs were surfacing.

Ralph went into the kitchen where the tub of dirty water sat surrounded by puddles and towels. Ralph stripped down to his underwear and washed himself. Feeling better, he sought his bed and sleep. As he drifted off he thought again of the ham, potatoes and pie that Elizabeth Yates had made. He knew that eating good food did not assuage all his yearnings. He wanted to feel what he'd felt for Bessie. Not just a woman that he could love and hold. He wanted to feel the excitement of being physically close. He did not want to just marry for need and convention alone. As much as he liked Elizabeth Yates, it was not love. There was no fire.

The days in Ralph's life just seemed to keep marching forward if he was ready for them or not. They got the pasture cleared on Friday and he decided they would take a day off and go to town on Saturday to visit Beverly. It was this visit to St. Joseph to see Beverly that made him realize she was becoming more attached to her adopted family. That gave Ralph divided feelings. He was glad she was comfortable but he felt some sadness and a loss too. Ralph still enjoyed the time there and as always, sorry to leave her behind. The Doc and his wife had embraced his little girl and Beverly was well because of it. Ralph felt no anger or rage. He was thankful for the help they extended. Beverly was beginning to conform to their way of life. He'd learned a long time ago that waves of hardship were often tossed with acts of kindness, and sometimes acts of kindness beget emotional pain.

They arrived home that night tired, but managed to get some supper eaten and their clothes ready for church the next morning. A breeze stirred and lightening skimmed across the sky. Ralph got his harmonica and went out to sit on the front porch. Betty and Lynn joined him and ran after lightening bugs. Ralph played one song after another tapping his foot to the faster ones. He felt lighthearted and gay for some reason. Maybe it was the weather or just the calm he always felt after seeing Beverly so healthy. For a moment he thought about that day at the cemetery wrestling with the decision to let the doc take Bev. He put down his mouth-harp and leaned over to catch a lightening bug himself. The old dog came up and lay at his feet. Ralph rubbed his back and the dog rolled over to nuzzle his hand. Me and you are two of a kind old boy, Ralph thought, just looking for someone to love us.

Lightning bolted into a tree somewhere not too far away. The cracking was followed by explosions of thunder. Betty and Lynn ran to the porch screaming. The dog crawled under the porch and Ralph jumped up as the rain began to pelt from the darkening sky. He opened the screen and the three of them rushed into the house as the wind began to blow rain through the door. Ralph didn't care. It was raining. Maybe the drought was over.

Darlene was reading a book and Nadine, who was sitting beside her on the couch mended a sock. Mary came down the stairs and went to the piano and began to pick out a song.

Ralph sat in his chair and pulled Betty in his lap. Lynn curled up on the couch next to Darlene and Nadine and they all listened to the rain. Ralph looked around at his babies and felt a great love for his family. He missed Bessie.

Chapter 7

I was growing really tired of being in the truck. The board seats were hard and getting more uncomfortable by the minute. The smell of sweat from too many of us cramped into one tight space had permeated my nostrils for good. At least the night was somewhat cooler. I could hear snoring coming from every corner. Too anxious to sleep, and knowing another chapter of my life was about to begin, memories of home tugged at my heart, while feelings of insecurity set up camp in my mind. Those grown-up feelings I'd sensed earlier appeared to have gotten lost somewhere along the way. Doubt and fear began to push away my confidence leaving feelings of uneasiness and dread. Some people, like Jack, are just born to adventure. He actually delighted in the unknown. Then there are people like me who are born to grasp the security of what they know. Two days ago I wasn't sure of even getting on this cattle truck and now I wasn't sure about getting off.

There's a lesson here, I thought, as I stared off into the darkness trying to think rationally.

I mulled over the direction my life had taken so quickly. I decided that a person must either step forward and embrace his future, working it like a piece of dough until it becomes acceptable or sit by and let that future lay flat, like biscuits that won't rise. I was somewhat amazed at myself and the ideas forming in my mind. Would my biscuits rise? I *did* make this trip even if pushed into it. This was a first step on the road to my future. I knew that I was beginning to mold the shape of my life.

I sighed, as the smell of a pig farm drifted into my nose and brought me back to the present.

Jack sat up rubbing his back. "My neck is getting stiff. I hope we're about there because I don't think I could ride a whole lot further."

"Me either." I confessed. "Do you smell the hogs?"

"I guess I do!" Jack rubbed his nose with the back of his hand.

"You guys awake?" Cody whispered through the dark quiet air.

"I can't sleep. Too excited I guess." I said.

"Me too," Cindy admitted. "I'm kind of nervous about getting there. What if they're mean?"

"If it doesn't work out, they'll be another place." Jack told them.

Others began to stir and stretch and look around to see where we were.

"Look off in the distance at them electric lights." Some one was pointing through the slats in the side of the truck. "That'd be Shenandoah."

Now everyone was awake and looking and talking about who'd done work at this farm before. Apparently the owner had a lot of land and could afford to hire out for help. Some seemed to think the drought hadn't hit Iowa so hard in the last year so the locals could work their own places and migrants were hired for some of the extra work. I listened. One man told about going to Zookspur, Iowa and working in the mines. He said they had camps with houses for the workers and the money wasn't bad if you didn't mind breathing the coal dust. The chatter of the men filled the truck as we neared our goal. I listened to all the information eager to grasp some understanding of my new occupation.

Everyone agreed that it had to be better than what Arkansas had to offer and though some of the workers on this truck did, at one time, think about heading west to California, most were content to try to stick it out in this area. After reading in the papers about all the camps being so overcrowded, men having to work for nothing more than pennies a day and seeing those photographs of families as miserable as the day they left the Midwest, it made you wonder if the whole world wasn't crumbling apart. We were lucky. Though we'd eaten beans and potatoes most every night back home, we did eat. I had not known true hunger. I hoped I never did.

All of a sudden the old truck jerked off the main highway, down a side road, and as we rounded a bend we could see some buildings with metal roofs that shimmered in the moonlight. The truckload of workers became quiet as we approached the farmstead, each trying to see what his future home looked like. But the night hid any real view of our destination. Cindy and I looked at each other and squeezed each other's hand. Cody and Jack were busy craning their necks with the other men. We felt the old truck brake. I was glad it had gotten us this far without incident. A screen door squeaked and slammed. Someone was coming toward us from the direction of the house, gleaming white amid the darkness of the night.

Dirk got up first, jerked up on the gate and jumped out, only turning around to grab his stuff.

"Point me to my bed, Grover." He said to the driver who was waiting on the ground at the back of the truck, ready for his cargo of people to unload.

"Jist wait yerself." The driver said impatiently.

The driver walked over to the man who had come from the big farm house. The moon gave enough light for me to see that he was older with white hair. They spoke a few minutes. Then our driver walked back to where our group was and the man went back toward the house.

When all of us were grounded with our possessions in hand, the driver pointed toward a barn and told the men that was where they would bunk. He told them that a bath house had been put up behind it and they'd find the bucket hanging on the cistern. He walked over to a shed, took a lantern off a hook, lit it and handed it to Jack.

"Son, lead the way. I'll get yer women settled in this little shed here. You men keep quiet and don't spook the horses. And, Dirk, stay away from the bottle." He lit another lantern and held it up high and looked at Cindy and me.

"You girls come on with me. Don't be scart none." He shuffled over toward the shed, as tired as the rest of us and maybe more so from the stress of driving.

Cindy and I looked at each other, then I turned to follow the man. Cindy looked at Cody.

"Cody, see you in the morning." Cindy said to him as they both hung back hesitant to part.

"Are you sure you'll be alright?" Cody asked not seeming very sure about it himself.

"Sure, they be alright." The old man told him. "They's a lock on the door and curtains on the winders. The missus fixed it up right nice the last time she had some women folk here. Might need an airin' out's the only thing."

Cody kissed Cindy gently, lingering for a moment, looking into her eyes. Then Cindy reached up, kissed him on the cheek and lightly smacked him on the backside.

"Go on to bed." She told him. "We'll be fine. You heard him."

Cody ran down to where the men were beginning to go into the barn.

We looked at the old man who had stopped a few yards ahead of us, beside the door of the little shed.

"Well are ya'll comin' or not?" He turned around and opened the door.

"We're coming." I said, and we walked quickly over

to the shed door.

"Here." He gave me the lantern. "There's a well out here and a bucket. You'll find a tub and a washbasin in there and soap on the cabinet. Be sure an lock the door."

We stepped inside and held up the lantern. The tub was there alright and there were four small cots. We turned back to the man but he was gone.

Putting our things down on the floor, we just stood there.

"I'll lock the door." I said, suddenly, realizing that we were really alone.

Cindy walked over and pushed a window open then went to the cabinet and opened the cupboards. She found some light blankets and pillows and tossed them onto the beds. We shook the dust from the stored linens and made up our beds.

"You want to pump some water and take a bath tonight?" Cindy asked.

"That would feel good, wouldn't it?" I was tired but so dirty.

"Let's get that bucket and at least get enough water to wash off." Cindy was already unlocking the door.

I followed her out after grabbing the lantern. She pumped as I held the light. When the bucket was full, she carried it inside and sloshed it into the tub. It was cool but we didn't care.

"Here." I told her handing over the lantern. "I'll do the next one."

We made three trips getting more excited every time. It felt so good to be out of the truck.

"You can go first." I told Cindy as I looked for towels. I found them and shook them out. Cindy was already in the tub splashing water around. I threw her a washrag and the soap. She began to laugh.

"Oh Johnnie Belle this feels so good." Cindy wasn't shy at all.

I put what few articles of clothing I'd brought into a small dresser, trying not to look at Cindy. I felt embarrassed but was determined that it would not stop me from climbing into that little tub. When I turned around, Cindy was standing in the tub dripping water, trying to get the small towel wrapped around her body. She looked at me.

"Oh, Johnnie Belle, Now don't you go and blush. We're both girls. Now me, I've never been shy. I guess that's because I have only sisters and my daddy was never around in the house much."

"Just one more thing I'll learn to overcome." I said, knowing it was a big mountain I was climbing but I wasn't going back now.

"Well go ahead, I'll get dressed for bed." Cindy made an effort to turn away and search through her sack to find her bedclothes. Then she busied herself putting her things into the same dresser.

"I am so tired." Cindy finished shutting the dresser drawers.

"Me too, but I feel a little nervous and wonder if I'll be able to sleep." As we spoke, I tried to slide down in the small tub of cool water, lathering my body with the lye soap.

"I think the bed will feel so good I'll probably fall asleep the minute I lay down." Cindy drew back the light cover, they'd just put on and sat down, testing the feel of the cot.

I stood up to dry off. My skin felt alive again. I pulled the flowered sackcloth towel around me as best I could and walked to my own bed where I'd left my bedclothes. Quickly dressing, I let the towel drop to the wooden floor. A mouse scurried across from the dresser towards the back wall.

"I hope we don't get too many visits from him." I said and laughed and lay down in my own small bed. Our house back in Star City had plenty of mice. One didn't frighten me.

"It's late." Cindy said.

"I know." I answered.

"Before I married Cody I'd never been away from home without being with one of my sisters." Cindy said more to herself than to me. "I can't decide if I'm excited or scared." She admitted.

"Me either." I rolled onto my side and looked at Cindy.

"Guess we'd better put out the lantern. Unlatch that other window and push it open, would you Johnnie Belle?" She jumped off her bed and I jumped off mine. I got the latch up and pushed the small wooden door that served as a window out to let in the still night air. Cindy put out the lantern and we both crawled into bed.

We lay there quietly for a long time, Cindy in her own world and me in mine.

"Cindy." I said quietly.

"What, Johnnie Belle." She whispered.

"Do you think that Dirk will make more trouble for us?"

"I don't know, but I'm going to stay out of his way for sure." Cindy rolled over on her side and looked at me.

"I think I'm ready to sleep now. Good-night Cindy."

"Good-night Johnnie Belle."

I lay there feeling strange, unsettled and alone. I don't know how long it was but I guess I fell asleep because the next thing I knew, I woke up in the dark, startled at my strange surroundings. Gathering my bearings, I listened wondering what woke me. My heart beat fast in my chest and I could hear Cindy's slow even breathing in the little room we shared. I could see the light of the moon across the sky and a few stars as I stared out through the open window. My imagination began to suggest dreadful possibilities and I grew quite awake. My anxieties overwhelmed me. I remembered the mouse and thought that's probably what I heard. Or the dog. It could have been the dog. Or a person. Maybe somebody was outside of our window or the door. I tried to calm my breathing thinking I was working myself up for no good reason.

I lay there still and silent for awhile afraid to move. Soon the quiet of the night became reassuring. Thinking there were probably all kinds of normal sounds on a farm at night, and adding that I was sleeping in a strange bed after a long trip, I convinced myself it was nothing. Once again I fell asleep until the sound of a rooster and the break of the new day nudged me back.

I sat up and looked around. The shed we were in didn't look like it'd hold up in a windstorm. I wondered how long it had been leaning. I hoped it was up to the struggle of staying upright, at least as long as we were there. Cindy was still sleeping. I decided to dress and go to the outhouse. The britches Mama had made for me to wear were in a heap on the floor beside the dirty tub of water. I pulled one of my three dresses over my head and put on my shoes. I combed my short hair back behind my ears, then quietly, trying not to wake Cindy, I unlocked the door and pushed it open a crack. It made a lot of noise and Cindy moved in her bed.

"That you, Johnnie Belle?" She asked sleepily.

"Yes. I'm going to the outhouse." I told her and pushed the door open all the way. A big old black dog ran over wagging its tail. I petted it, but walked on. The dog followed me. I knocked on the door and stood there for a moment with the dog nuzzling my leg. Guessing no one was in it, I slowly opened the door and went in. When I came out the dog was still there. I was used to dogs. We never had one but Star City was full of dogs and I didn't mind them at all. This one was sure friendly enough. Together we walked back to the leaning shed which was now my home. When I opened the door, Cindy was sitting up. She grinned at me as I tried to get the door shut without catching the dog's nose.

"Found a friend I see." She mused.

"Well, he found me. I think he woke me up last night. Probably chasing a rabbit under the floorboards or something." I thought about that.

"What do you mean?" Cindy asked.

"Well, I woke up in the night. I thought I heard something. But I didn't hear it again. It was probably the dog or my imagination." I explained.

"You should have called out to me." Cindy told me as she got up and dressed herself.

"You were sleeping. Anyway, I guess it was nothing but my own jitters. You want to help me dump the water?"

Cindy grabbed one side of the metal tub and we sloshed toward the door where we both set it down while I unlatched the lock.

"Ready?" I looked at Cindy.

"Yes." She replied and she followed as I pushed the door open and backed out into the dirt yard. The old dog began to lap at the water.

"Get on out of here." I fussed at him smiling.

We got the tub to the side of the shed and tipped it up. We stood watching the water soak into the hungry ground, the dog fighting to get a share.

"I'll put it back in." Cindy said. "You want to fill the bucket for us?"

"Sure." I said rubbing the back of the dog who had decided that we would be companions for the day.

The water was cold this morning but felt good and woke me up. I hung my towel and wash rag on a nail that was in the board beside the washstand.

"I'm hungry. I wonder how we get breakfast." Cindy looked out the window then turned to find her own comb and wash her own face.

When we had made our beds, we left the shed to face the day. Cindy went to the outhouse and I looked around at Iowa.

The first thing I noticed was that it was nearly as flat as home. The land stretched out for miles with only a few rolling slopes. Far off I saw a line of trees that marched in a curved pattern down through a shallow valley. I figured it was a river that sustained the growth. There were a couple of tall shade trees close to the house, but the rest was all farmland. I hadn't ever seen so much field space in all my life. Rows and rows of crops that I did not recognize neatly planted and cared for, stood waiting, but for what I did not know. There was no cotton here, and I had never seen any cotton field that was near as big as one of these. I sat down on what remained of a pile of wood and the old dog came over to lie at my feet. The sunrise spread across the smooth ground like butter across a pancake, melting and oozing ever so slowly and mixing with the colors of the earth. Men began to amble up from the barn and towards the house. A few chickens pecked at the dirt looking for bugs. Just then a door banged.

A man had emerged from the big farmhouse and was coming in my direction. I leapt up, keeping my eyes down.

"Breakfast in the kitchen. Beth is a layin' it out now. Just go on in the back door there and you'll find a wash basin." He walked on towards the men coming up from the barn.

Cindy came out of the outhouse and over to where I was standing, tongue-tied and red in the face. "What's the matter?"

"Nothing," I said embarrassed that I could get so rattled just because a man I did not know had approached me. "The man of the house said to go on in that door, there, to the kitchen, wash up and eat breakfast. He said his wife, Beth was laying it out now."

"Then let's go." Cindy took my hand and we walked to the old screen door. The chickens were gathering around some scattered corn but they scurried in all directions as we passed.

We knocked lightly.

"Come on in. No need to knock." A woman from inside yelled back at us.

We went in and spotted the wash pan and washed our hands.

"Hello." Cindy called out peeking from the porch into the kitchen unsure about just walking into somebody's house.

"Come on in, sit down and eat up. No need to waste yer time." She was pulling biscuits from the stove.

We sat down and she pushed a bowl of gravy over. "Go ahead. Help yerselves. You drink coffee?"

"Thank you. No, we don't drink coffee." Cindy said again since it appeared I had lost my voice.

We both took a biscuit and poured gravy over it. Then she put down a platter of bacon and eggs and we each took some.

"Now eat up cause there won't be anything more till 12:00 noon. That's eatin' time up here. Supper at seven or eight, depending on the field work." She continued to open and close the stove, which already created a rise in the temperature of the kitchen.

Cindy and I looked at each other, and then helped ourselves to the eggs and bacon.

"You might as well drink all the milk you can hold cause we milk our own cows."

We did. Some of the men drifted in, sat down and helped themselves.

"Mornin' there Al. Good to see you again." She said to one of the men.

"How are ya' ma'am?" Al asked her tipping his hat.

"Now Al, you take that hat clear off in this house. You know my rules."

"Yes ma'am." He drawled and put his hat on the floor beside his chair.

"Now you girls finish up so some others can have your places and we'll get everybody fed and out to work before 6:30 comes around." She never stopped moving.

"Well, Missus Beth, it's been a long time." One of the men went over and gave her a hug.

"Henry Jones! Thought we'd seen the last of you. How's the wife?" Beth asked as Cindy and I got up and cleared our dishes while listening to the banter between those who had been up here before and the woman who appeared to run the house.

"Well, ma'am, she didn't make it. Kids are all married so I decided to come back again." Henry Jones hung his head.

"I'm so sorry." The woman said comforting him. "Sit down now and have some breakfast. You must be hungry."

"That I is." Henry Jones said as he sat down and began to help himself to large quantities of food.

Cindy and I moved back through the door and into the ever rising light of the day. Cody and Jack were just coming up from the barn.

Cindy ran to meet them and gave Cody a big hug and a kiss. As they came up to where I was, I smiled.

"Sleep alright?" Jack asked.

"Yes." I said. "How about you?"

"Like a log." He stretched and yawned.

"The farmer's wife is inside serving breakfast now. We already ate. You two better go in before things get low." I pointed to the screen door where men continued to go in and out as they had their breakfast. "It was good and filling. Sounds like we'll be working it off in no time though."

"Let's go Cody." Jack headed for the kitchen smells then turned around. "The dinner bell rings when it's time to meet out here to go to the fields.

"Ok. We'll be here." I said.

"Let's go back to our bunks till then." Cindy said.

We walked over and opened the door, leaving it ajar while we waited for the bell to sound. We both lay across our beds and sighed.

"I wonder what we'll do today." I said, more to myself than to Cindy.

"Me too," She said softly. "I'm just glad we're not getting back on that truck."

"Have you ever seen such a farm?" I asked Cindy as I sat up and gazed out the window at the rows in the field.

"Not me." She said.

Suddenly the old dinner bell rang. We looked at each other desperately. Jumping up, we got our old hats out and put them on. We weren't either one too concerned with how we looked but had worked enough cotton to know that wearing a hat made a lot of difference in how we took the heat...

"Are you ready?" She asked.

"No." I replied honestly. "But let's go anyway."

We walked out the door putting our hats on and headed in the same direction as the men. Some were still coming from the kitchen with biscuits in hand. The farmer was there to meet us.

"We got work to do." The farmer began. His accent sounded funny. He sure didn't talk normal like us anyway. "I'm going to divide you up in crews, appoint leaders and hand out your assignments for the day. Everybody gets paid minus room and board at the end of each week. Same rules as last year. No drinkin' on the farm. Save it for the pool hall in town. No fights and if ya' rile my Missus you're fired. I expect ya to work hard and give me my money's worth. Stay clear of the horses and mules unless you're trained to work 'em. Any questions?" He stood there looking around at us. Then pulled a paper from his pocket and began to put us into three crews.

I felt sick and wondered how I'd cope if I didn't get in with Cindy or Jack. Cindy squeezed my hand. I looked at her. I knew she understood what I was thinking. Finally he began dividing us up. Thankfully, Jack, Cody, Cindy and I all ended up in the same group. What a relief that was. About as much as learning that Dirk was not in our group. He was in the group that would work with the team of horses. The farmer finished telling us what to do, how to work, and where to go. He said to head on out, that he'd be there directly to show us exactly how to do it the way he wanted. We were going to start cutting corn and tying it into shocks. We headed around to the other side of the men's barn where he said the corn fields were. He said it was a mite early but if he didn't cut it now it would dry up anyhow. We believed that.

As we walked the short distance I saw a group of men with Dirk leading the way, heading toward the big barn where the horses were probably kept. I looked around at the land. It didn't matter in which direction I looked; I could not see another house. Another dog ran across the back yard and I saw an old swing hanging from a large old apple tree. There was a small hill with a door that went right into the ground where the cellar must have been. Beyond that was a clothes line tied from the house to a pole. Further over was a vegetable garden that didn't look too healthy. A cow bawled somewhere in the distance and I got another whiff of pigs coming from over that north rise. I liked this big farm. I felt a contentment being in a place that could provide so much. I'd like to live on a farm one day. Back home, most of my enjoyment, besides reading books, came from working in Mama's garden. Having a milk cow would be nice.

We all headed toward the cornfield and stood around waiting for the farmer. Two men in our group appeared to have been here before. They went to retrieve some tools from the small barn where the men had slept. We all watched the men from the other group come out of the big barn with large work horses. They began hitching them to some piece of farm equipment. Finally the farmer appeared to give us direction and we began to work. Cindy and I carried shocks of corn that others had cut and we laid it in piles near the barn. Later they would be tied up and stored on end.

The morning was nice, but, as predicted, we were all stiff from riding so nobody moved too quickly. Every so often we got drinks from the dipper in a bucket of water. The men often poured the water over their heads to cool off, but Cindy and I refrained.

The morning progressed and the heat level rose. No breeze meant no relief from the ever mounting sun. Our arms scorched through the sweat and dirt that clung tightly to our skin. When the water bucket was empty, Cindy and I took turns going to the pump and getting more. It seemed a very long morning before we heard the dinner bell calling us to the noon meal. Our group eyed each other with relief and did not hesitate. At the cistern, we all washed up as best we could. Cindy and I decided to stop by our shed to comb our hair. Most everyone else headed toward the kitchen door.

I took my wash rag and dipped it in the lukewarm water and washed my face. Cindy pulled her hair out of the ponytail and brushed it. I put my rag back on its nail and picked up my own comb. My hair was thin and, after Mama had cut it, I did not need a brush. Knowing we could not all sit at the table at one time, Cindy and I decided to lay down for a moment and eat with the second group. We could smell the food and our stomachs growled at our decision. Our legs, arms, and backs, though, seemed glad for the rest.

Finally we heard the screen door banging. Men were coming out from the first shift, so we got up. Both of us moved stiffly, almost like old women. We might as well get used to this I thought looking up at the sun as I walked outside. Cindy followed me, gently pushing the door to, careful not to send our abode trembling into a heap. We met Cody and Jack by the door to the kitchen, since they had waited the same as we had. We all walked in pausing in the porch area to wash. The food smelled so good.

Cody let Cindy and me go into the kitchen first and Jack followed. We sat with the others and began to pass the dishes of food around. Our respite was too short. Before we were really ready, we were back outside and headed for the fields. We didn't do much talking because it just made us thirstier. It was too hot to care about anything other than getting the work done. By the end of the day, Cindy and I once again looked forward to a cool bath and bed.

Mornings were hard because of sore muscles and blistered hands. By the end of the first week we were ready for a break. We were let off from work mid-afternoon on Saturday. We did not have to go back to work until Monday morning.

And we got paid. The farmer and his wife were headed into town to shop and offered to give anyone of us a ride. Jack, Cody, Cindy and I decided we'd rather walk the few miles than to ride in the back of a truck again so soon.

After cleaning up, we met under the big tree in the back yard and began our excursion. Small groups of men were scattered along the road, some in front of us and some behind us all heading in the same direction, with the same purpose in mind - a change of scenery. The sun was hot, but I refused to wear the old work hat Mama had sent with me. It was nice to just stroll along, with no worry about being told to hurry.

The four of us talked about all the ways to spend our money. Ice cream seemed to top the list. We wondered about a movie and how much it would cost. Cindy and Cody did not intend to spend much of their money but to save it instead.

The road was dusty and dry. A gentle breeze was welcome though it stirred up the dust. It was different than Arkansas. Off in the distance far to the south, I could see another farmstead that rose in the middle of the fields with only one tree to shade its occupants. Other than that there was nothing to hold our attention. It wasn't long before we were wondering how much further the town could be and wishing that we had taken the farmer up on his offer of a ride.

About the same time we thought we were too tired to walk another step, a little rise in the road brought the town up ahead into our view. The sight spurred us on. The town looked to be bustling with activity. At every turn we saw men from our crew.

"I want to post this letter first." I was waving my second letter to Mama.

"Over there." Cindy pointed down the street to a sign on a building. "I'll go with you."

"Cody, there's a place to get ice cream. We'll meet

you two over there in just a minute." Cindy told him.

"Alright," Cody agreed. He and Jack walked across the street dodging a truck and a car to get there.

Cindy and I walked on down the sidewalk to send my letter. Ambling slowly we gazed in every window, admiring the many items offered for sale.

"I've never had money of my own to spend on anything I pleased." I said excitedly.

"Me either." Cindy replied walking up to the next large window and pressing her face up against the glass, shading her eyes with her hands. "Look at that."

I moved beside her and copied her stance to see what it was. She was looking at an unusual style of dress displayed on a plastic model of a woman.

"Where would you wear such a dress?" I asked.

"To a fancy party or a dance," Cindy said, obviously knowing more about these things than I did.

She finally pulled away from the window and looked around.

"Let's mail that letter and meet the boys." She was looking at me but I could see from her eyes that her mind was still dwelling on that dress.

"You know, Cindy, you could go back in and try it on." I smiled at her and at myself for thinking of something so daring.

"Do you think I should?" She brightened and really looked at me.

"I don't see why not. We could come back after we eat ice cream."

"I'll give it some thought." Cindy said calmly with stars in her eyes.

We headed in the direction of the ice cream parlor evading a team of horses pulling a wagon as we crossed the street. We jumped up onto the sidewalk and walked to a little shop that had red gingham curtains in the windows. Opening the door we could see the boys already settled at the corner table and were halfway through what looked like root-beer floats.

"Have a seat, ladies." Jack got up and held a chair for me. It was all show, but I let it pass. Cody did the same for Cindy.

"Where have you two been?" Cody asked.

"We were looking at a dress in a window." Cindy told him. "I might go back to try it on. Just for fun that is. I know we can't afford new things like that now. But it would be fun just to try it on."

"Why don't you order your ice cream and we'll talk about it." Cody suggested.

The waitress walked over and took our order. I ordered strawberry ice cream in a dish and Cindy ordered a coke float. We waited and watched the boys eat theirs slowly, relishing every spoonful and slurping the last bits through a straw just as ours arrived.

"Well girls, what is the plan for the afternoon. We hear there's a dance tonight over at the social hall. Do you want to stick around for that?"

Cindy and I looked at each other.

"Yes!" We said excitedly in unison.

"I've never been to a dance." I said.

"Cody and I used to go to the barn dances north of Star City. We'd square dance." Cindy scooted closer to Cody and he put his arm around her and gave her a kiss.

"Well, looks like that's settled." Jack said. "It's 3:00

now. Why don't we meet at that little cafe at about six and have a bite to eat, then walk on over to the social hall. The dance starts at seven."

"Maybe Johnnie Belle and I will go back over to look at that dress again." Cindy looked at Cody.

"Maybe I should come and see you in this dress." He smiled.

"Oh, I don't know." Cindy said flirting with her husband.

"I'd like to." Cody smiled at Cindy.

Watching them made me smile. Cody was so gentle, kind and loving toward Cindy. I couldn't help but feel some envy about having someone think I was so special. Cindy was lucky. I wondered if she would rather go alone with Cody. Maybe she was just being nice to include me. I knew they needed time together after spending most of the week living in separate places.

"You know, Cindy, I think I'll go over to that sewing shop and look at the cloth and buttons they have. You and Cody go on together. I'll meet you back at the cafe at six."

"Are you sure, Johnnie Belle? You could surely come along with us. We wouldn't mind a bit. Would we Cody?" Cindy shook her head and looked at me.

"Johnnie Belle, we'd be mighty pleased to have your company." Cody said sincerely.

"Thank you both but I really want to see the prices of that cloth and this would give me time to wander through the store and do some dreaming of my own."

I scooted back my chair and stood to go. "I'll see you both later. Bye, Jack." I waved and headed out the door gaining confidence with each passing minute.

"Bye." Cindy said. "See you at six."

As the door closed behind me, a little bell that was attached to the doorknob tinkled softly. I strolled toward the fabric shop looking at the people, the shops and the traffic in the street. Shenandoah was definitely a bigger town than Star City. I wondered if any of these women did washing and cleaning like Mama. I wondered if there were hungry people here. The people on the street did not appear to have much more money than we had back home if you went by their clothes. Most of the men were in overalls that were clean but patched and women were in work dresses similar to the ones I wore. I put my hand up to smooth back my hair. It was straight and I was trying to let it grow so I could pull it back into a ball, out of the way. As I passed people I looked down too shy to meet their looks. Every once in awhile I met a man from our crew and I would say hello. I'd gotten to know about everyone's name and, except for Dirk, they seemed alright.

The fabric store window was blooming with the colors of summer mixed with some fall prints. I looked for a moment before entering to feast on the soft melon colors that mixed with the pale greens and blues. Blue was my favorite color. It brought out my hazel eyes better than any other. I liked the pale shades, but Mama always said I looked better in darker hues. I went in.

"Hello." A shopkeeper called from somewhere in the back. "We'll be closing in thirty minutes."

"Thank you." I called back and began to wander through the bolts of cloth that were stacked according to types of fabric. I was attracted to the floral patterns. I touched them and dreamed of sewing up a dress in one of those pieces. I had never purchased new cloth for a dress. Mama always got hand-me-downs from people she worked for and remade them for me. By then the colors had usually faded and were old looking. Someday, I thought I'm going to buy some new material and make myself a brand new dress. I thought about Cindy looking at the fancy dress across the street. I did not care about having a fancy dress; just a new one. With so many sisters, I was sure that Cindy's mother made new dresses from time to time. They would certainly get used as each girl grew into them. It must have been fun having so many sisters.

I was standing there dreaming when the sales lady came up to me. "May I help you with something?" She asked.

"Oh, no, thank you." I said. "I was just looking."

"Well, we close in a few minutes so if you want to make a purchase you need to make up your mind." The woman was quickly folding up pieces that had been unrolled by other shoppers who had been looking. I expected she was tired and ready to go home. I decided to leave.

"Good-by." I said as I headed toward the door.

"Good-by." She said, then looked up at me as though really noticing me for the first time and said, "Have a nice evening. Are you going to the dance at the social hall?"

I looked back at her surprised at her interest. "Yes ma'am." I replied.

"You sound like you're from the South." She smiled.

"Yes ma'am, I am." I said. "Thank you again for letting me look around. Your material is right nice."

"Any time young lady. You come back anytime."

I closed the door and sighed. She was nice, I thought. I walked towards the cafe. I was early and decided to sit on the bench that was in front of the cafe to wait. Looking around, I saw Dirk. He was coming up an alley drinking from a bottle. I looked in the other direction hoping he would not see me. Then I saw Cindy and Cody walking my way. I jumped up and walked quickly toward them and we all went into the cafe. We sat at a table where Jack joined us. We ordered, ate, and chatted away comparing stories about our various adventures.

Though we had all been tempted, none of us spent any of our small wages. We all knew how hard that money was to come by and none of us was anxious to give it up.

When we were finished eating, we walked to the social hall. It stood out of town on the road that led toward the farm. We saw a few of the men from our camp standing around outside of the building. Others were heading on back down the road toward what was our current home. We could hear the music coming from inside and walked in slowly, taking in the new surroundings. Farmers and their wives were waltzing to a soft tune played by a fiddler and another man with a guitar. A harmonica player stood up, put his instrument to his mouth and began to accompany them. It was about the nicest moment I'd had since leaving Arkansas. The music captured something inside me and I wished it would hold me forever. Couples swayed and moved around the small floor while others stood visiting with each other or just sat listening to the tunes that floated through the oppressive heat in the room.

Jack grabbed my hand and pulled me to the floor.

"I can't dance." I told him horrified.

"I'll teach you." He held me loosely and told me not to look at my feet.

"Just follow what I do." He said.

I felt my face getting hot with embarrassment.

"Johnnie Belle, loosen up." Jack said.

"I can't." I told him. "I'm embarrassed to death."

"Well don't be. Look at the others. Everyone's having a nice time and no one is even looking at us."

I looked around and saw that he was right and relaxed a little. I saw Cindy and Cody dancing and they looked terrific. Just as I was thinking I might actually enjoy dancing, the music stopped. Everyone clapped. Immediately the little group started playing again, but this time it was a fast song and Jack began to jump around. He grabbed my hand and started to swing me. A man was calling this one. I felt the beat, took a few steps, mimicking Jack and decided I liked this faster tune. I did not move quite as wildly as Jack but I was catching on little by little. What would mama say if she saw us flying across a dance floor? She'd think I'd plum gone crazy, though not Jack. She would expect Jack to be enjoying a barn dance. I thought that mama would be proud of me.

Finally, the group took a break. The four of us decided to walk outside to get some fresh air. We were happy and laughing, though I was still trying to get over the feeling that other people were looking at me.

"Johnnie Belle, I thought you said you'd never danced before." Cindy laughed happily, her own face red from exercise, the heat and the week of being in the sun.

"It was my first time." I said shyly wondering what she would say about my clumsy movements.

"You couldn't tell by me." She said.

"Thanks." I said gratefully.

"Well, if it ain't the pretty little ladies from Arkansas." Dirk had stumbled out behind us, drunk.

"Leave us alone, Dirk." Cody said.

Cindy and I moved back. Jack and Cody stood their ground while the dark man moved closer to them.

"I'll do whatever I want to." He slurred and took another drink from the bottle in his hand.

"Dirk, leave 'em be." One of the other men from the crew grabbed Dirk's arm to pull him back.

Dirk turned around and shoved him back then lunged at Jack and Cody.

Cindy screamed. I just stood petrified, afraid to move. He caught Jack and Cody off guard and they both went sprawling. Dirk was over to where Cindy and I were standing within seconds. He grabbed me and I heard myself screaming for Jack. I was pushed against the wall. He put his arms around mine trying to kiss me. I struggled trying to get away still, screaming for Jack.

"You've been askin' for this ever since you got on the truck, givin' them looks and actin' so shy."

All of a sudden he let go of me. I fell to the ground. When I looked up, I realized that Jack had him down on the ground and was punching him in the face.

"Stop, Jack." I screamed. I knew when Jack got mad he could be hard to stop.

Some men grabbed Jack off Dirk, holding him until he quit struggling. Dirk lay in the dirt. He looked dead.

"Jack. You killed him." I whispered hoarsely. "Nah, he didn't." One of the men said laughing. "But he plugged him up perty good."

I looked over at Cindy. Cody was holding her. She looked at me and put her hand to her mouth.

"Johnnie Belle, your dress!" She looked shocked.

I looked down and saw that my dress was torn. I looked at Jack. He was wiping his clothes off. He looked over at me, took his shirt off and gave it to me to wear over my torn dress.

It was all over. The happy moment. The music. The dancing. And probably, our job. It swept across me in one motion. What would we do now?

I looked at Cindy and Cody and Jack. Somebody found some water and threw it on Dirk. He sputtered to life, but Jack had done a job on him. His face was cut and bloodied. He weaved off not even looking in our direction.

"Let's head home." Cody said.

We all turned and headed back to the farm. None of us spoke. I shivered, as my mind relived the violent moment at the dance. Walking would give us time to think and calm down. I decided that I would not let Dirk spoil the whole day for me. Looking up at the darkening sky, seeing the first stars shining down on our path. I knew they were the same stars I looked at back home. It made me feel like home was not quite so far away. If I just kept looking up instead of out to the unending fields, I could pretend I was home in my bed, gazing out my window, with Mama in the other room. It calmed me and I took a deep breath of the fresh night air. The wind was coming up and lightning broke behind a cloud far to the north. Heat lightning, we called it back home It seemed the heavens could not spare even a bit of rain to settle the dust that scattered under our feet. As we walked quietly down the road, Cindy took my hand and squeezed it. I looked back at her and smiled gratefully. We all knew that the events of the evening signaled a change to come.

Chapter 8

From habit Ralph woke up every day of his life at dawn, ready to do chores, eat breakfast, and get to work. It was no different on that Monday morning. He was at the wash basin in the kitchen shaving when Nadine came down. She sat sleepily at the kitchen table not saying a word. Ralph finished shaving, wiped his face and combed his black hair towards the back on both sides of the part that worked its way down the center of his head. It was a hair style that fit him. He walked over to the stove, picked up a piece of cornbread, and then pulled a jar of milk from the ice box. He set the milk and bread on the table and got himself a glass from the cupboard. Back at the table, he poured a glass of milk then mashed his cornbread down into the glass, mixing it all together. He returned the milk to the icebox and sat down. With a big spoon he began ladling the mixture into his mouth. Nadine sat looking out of the window at the sky which was getting lighter by the moment.

Ralph knew that he'd have to be on his way soon to get all the way to Clarinda. He had a big day. First he needed to get that load of sweet corn, deliver it, then pick up the hogs and haul them back south to St. Joe. Hopefully he'd get home again in time to eat supper with the family. He had an uncomfortable feeling that something was on Nadine's mind. Whenever one of the girls made an effort to catch him alone he knew he would be confronted with something bigger than whose turn it was to do the dishes. Ralph preferred to deal with the basics in life.

Aunt Ruth had been pretty handy about being there for the girls when they needed a woman to talk to, but there were times when he and the girls just had to jump right into the middle of a situation.

Nadine looked at him and he looked at her. He could talk to strangers anywhere, about anything, but he sure had trouble when it came to talking one on one with his girls.

"Dad," Nadine finally said, though not looking at him.

"What is it?" He said trying to sound as detached as he could, hoping for a subject he might be able to deal with, and once again questioned God as to why Bessie had to die.

"Dad," Nadine began again. "Can I go out sometimes when I live with Mrs. Baxter or do I have to stay with her all the time when I'm not in school?"

Ralph smiled. He could deal with this.

"Nadine, Mrs. Baxter is frail, but not nearly dead. If a nice boy asks you to step out you can go. You're old enough to not have to ask permission. Just let Mrs. Baxter know ahead of time. Be fair with her and make sure she doesn't need you first." Ralph looked at her.

"Is that all, Nadine?" He asked hoping it was but sure it was not.

"Yes." She nodded, and then continued quickly. "Duane Cobb has been talking to me at church. He asked if he could take me to the movies next Saturday. I really want to go, but I wasn't sure since I'll be at Mrs. Baxter's house."

"Nadine, life won't stop just because you go to school or live somewhere else. It just keeps on moving along. You'll find that out soon enough. You and Mrs. Baxter will have to learn how to work things out between you, but you're a grown girl now and you're going to have to make decisions on your own. You know right from wrong. Use your head and think before you do anything." Ralph got up and walked to the back door, put his hat on his head, then pushed it back.

"You remind me of your Mother, Nadine." Ralph was always seeing some of Bessie in his girls. "I've got a long way to travel today. I'll try to be home for supper. If I'm late, eat without me. Aunt Ruth said she might get out today and help you pack if you need it. Invite her to stay over for supper, if she comes, will you?"

"Sure Daddy." Nadine said. "I'm about done packing but I hope Aunt Ruth comes anyway. She always lets me take her hair down and braid it. Have you ever seen how long her hair is?"

"Not for a long time. I'm leaving now. I'll be back when I can." Ralph left through the back porch and walked out to the truck. The morning was already humid but he felt good. It was hard to believe how fast his girls were growing. Next thing you know they'll all be getting married and having families of their own. That idea caught his attention. Ralph could not imagine not having a house full of children to come home to. It was something he had not thought about and it made him feel a little sad. He loved his family more than anything. His family and his work was all he knew. He got into the truck and threw his hat onto the dirty seat. Starting up the truck he backed it out onto the road. As he pulled away to start his day, the lonely feeling lifted. He liked his work. It wasn't being gone from home, or away from the children that he enjoyed so much, but more that he would be driving through the country he knew so well, the wind in his face, watching the shape of each farm with it's crops struggling to thrive and cattle grazing upon the hillsides. He loved farming and all it demanded of him. Farming was not only physically hard, but you had to be smart about what and when you planted. In a couple of years he hoped he'd be able to sell his land and buy another farm that he could work and improve. The drought couldn't last forever and farming would once again be profitable. But for now he'd have to be satisfied with part-time farming and trucking. Ralph understood the ups and downs of life and was biding his time while he watched the world's struggle with weather and poverty. He was smart. He worked hard. He persevered. He stayed afloat when others went under.

Ralph picked up his load of sweet corn and headed north toward Clarinda. It would be midmorning before he got to the Grove farm and Annie Grove would have hot sticky buns fresh from the stove about then. He enjoyed the Groves. George and Annie had been friends since they were young and he was always glad for the work they gave him. He knew that it helped them out, and it sure had helped him to keep food on his own table.

Pulling into the Patterson's filling station, Ralph put gasoline into his tank and bought a bottle of orange pop.

"Hey, Ralph." A voice from under the hood of an old truck yelled at him.

"That you, Jacob?" Ralph asked.

"Yeah." Jacob Patterson came out of the shed wiping his greasy hands on his overalls. "Where ya' headed?"

"Clarinda. Got this load of sweet corn to deliver to Delbert's store and Grove's hogs to pick up and take to St. Joe."

"Say, there's a hitch-hiker down at the crossroads cafe. Came through here about thirty minutes ago. He's headed up north. Say's he's got family up in Des Moines. You might give him a lift part-ways anyway." Jacob headed back into the shed and put his head back into the engine of the truck. "I told him I'd send any rides his way. "

"Glad to help." Ralph nodded, took the money for the gasoline out of his coin purse, went into the station and laid it on the counter.

"Thanks for your business, Ralph." Patterson hollered.

"Take care now, Jacob." Ralph said as he got into his own truck and headed down the road.

As he neared the crossroads he slowed and pulled into the little cafe. Ralph grabbed his hat, jumped out and went inside, leaving the truck door swinging. He was moving on with his day and would not be slowed down.

"Somebody here want a ride as far as Clarinda?" He asked, pushing his hat back and rubbing his forehead.

A man jumped up from a chair and stuck out his hand. "Vernon Polk."

Ralph met his hand. "Ralph Showalter. Let's go. My truck's running."

The man grabbed his bag and hustled out to the waiting vehicle glad to get a ride.

"I appreciate the ride Mister." Vernon Polk responded.

"Glad to do it." Ralph told him motioning him to his truck. "Where you from? Sound like you're from the south."

"I'm from south Missouri." Polk told Ralph. Both men slammed their doors and put their elbows on the window. "I'm headed towards Des Moines. Got kinfolk there. I'm hoping they kin hep me to find work." Polk stretched his left arm over the back of the seat. "Ain't got no family. Jist on my own. You got family?"

Ralph could tell already the man was a talker. He picked up hitch-hikers on a regular basis and usually enjoyed their company on trips.

"I've got seven babies." Ralph told him, always proud to talk about his family.

"Seven babies?" The man gaped.

"Well," Ralph smiled. "They're not really babies, but they're all my babies if you know what I mean.

Ralph drove as fast as the old truck could be prodded with the load.

"Now I agree with that. Seems like just yesterday I was a boy, and now, here I am a grown man travelin' and lookin' fer work." Polk smiled and sat up a little straighter as if to emphasize his manhood.

"My oldest girl, Nadine is leaving this week to go to college." Ralph thought about Nadine and their conversation that morning.

"How many girls you got?" The man asked.

"Five." Ralph told him. "And two boys."

"Your wife must be a plum busy lady." He laughed and looked at Ralph.

"My wife died five years ago." Ralph told him.

"I'm sorry." Polk shook his head. "How do you take care of all of em'?"

"The older ones all help out. My sisters help some. And sometimes I take my little boy on trips with me. This next year though he'll be in school and I'm figuring I'll have to stay home more." He thought about Beverly. It was not something he could discuss with a stranger. "I got me a few acres and I'm hoping this drought is letting up so I can farm a good crop or two."

"Sounds like you need to get married again." Vernon Polk offered his advice.

"I've been told that." Ralph pondered. "Just haven't met the right woman. Say you wouldn't be interested in a job to help me with some acreage I just purchased, would you? I could use a good hand for a few weeks.'

"Naw, I got to get up to Des Moines. There's a factory job there pays good wages and my sister is expectin' me any time. I ain't no farmer."

"Well, just asking." Ralph thought it was too bad. He could use the help so the girls could stay at home with the younger ones and keep up the house chores. He'd hoped Ralph Wendell would farm with him but he was more interested in working on car engines. He'd get along. He always had. They sat in silence for a long spell enjoying the breeze created by the speed of the truck.

"How much further is it to Clarinda?" The man asked.

"About another hour," Ralph told him.

"Do you care if I nap?" Vernon Polk took his hat off and put it on the torn seat.

Ralph looked at him and realized he'd probably walked quite a piece. His face was sunburned and weary. He was not very big or muscular. "Don't mind at all." Ralph replied.

The man scooted down in the seat and put his head back against the window. It wasn't five minutes before he was snoring, his mouth hanging open and catching the breeze. Ralph hit a bump in the road a little harder than needed and Vernon Polk shut his mouth. Ralph smiled.

Ralph enjoyed the quiet as he drove on to Clarinda. The town was set against small sloping hills with dry and sparse corn fields struggling in the heat. If you didn't grow corn up here you were a dairy farmer with a few hogs on the side. One look at Clarinda and you knew life here wasn't much better than anywhere else. The buildings lacked paint, too many men stood around in their overalls just holding up the place. Not enough work. It wasn't any wonder Vernon Polk was heading for the city and factory work. Ralph pulled into another filling station to get gasoline, a drink, and fill up the water in his radiator. Mr. Polk woke up when he stopped the truck.

"We here?" He asked.

"We're in Clarinda." Ralph told him. "As soon as I deliver this load of corn to Delbert's Grocery, I've got to head out West a few miles to the Grove farm. You're welcome to ride out there with me."

"Naw, I'd better be a gittin' on north. But I thank ya'

fer the ride, Mister." Vernon Polk opened the door of the truck and pulled his bag out. He grabbed his hat and put it on his head. "Thanks again for the ride." Polk stuck out his hand toward Ralph.

Ralph shook his hand and surveyed the young man. He thought Polk looked a little worse for wear, but he was young and he'd get over it once he was settled and had some sleep.

"You're welcome," Ralph told him as Polk dropped his hand and headed back toward the main northbound road. Ralph watched him wondering just how old he was. After he finished filling the tank, Ralph walked into the little shack of a station, grabbed a root beer, and paid the man standing there. He picked up a toothpick that was in a little holder on the counter and stuck it in his mouth while he walked back to the truck. Getting in he slammed the door and cranked the engine. It smoked and backfired. Ralph let it set a moment and tried it again.

"Look's like it could use a little engine work." A man from the station came out to sit on the curb.

"Probably could." Ralph said and gave it another try. This time it started right up and he let out on the clutch, rolling slowly away from the gas pump and back into the street. He drank the root beer, headed towards Delbert's store. He backed up his truck and Francis Snyder came out to help with the unloading. Ralph went inside to settle up. He might have stood around and talked with some of the others, but he was focused on heading west, out of town towards the Grove's place, and thought he could smell homemade sweet rolls already.

As Ralph approached the Groves dairy farm he thought it looked as neglected as everyone else's place. He pulled up to the front of the house and saw George out near the barn getting the loading chute set up to load the hogs. Swinging around, and throwing the truck into reverse he backed the rear end down that way until he was close and turned off the key. As usual, Ralph jumped out and left the door open. He reached out to ruffle the thick matted fur of George's old cattle dog. Ralph couldn't remember a time when old Burl wasn't a part of the Grove's family.

"Hello." Ralph called out.

"Hi there, Ralph." George Grove waved with his gloved hand. "Don't come out here, let's go inside and have some of Annie's rolls and coffee first."

"Won't get any argument from me," Ralph laughed as George swung over the fence and shook Ralph's hand. The hogs squealed and snorted and rutted through the mud for the last potato peelings. George smelled as bad as the pig lot.

"Say George, you ever take a bath?" Ralph teased.

"Never," George smiled back. "How ya' been, Ralph?" George asked him.

"Pretty good, considering we haven't had any more rain than you have. Thought we'd get a gully washer the other night, but it stopped about as soon as it started."

George shook his head back and forth and looked serious. "I might have to sell if things don't turn around soon."

"Well, I just bought a few acres to farm thinking it would turn around." Ralph told him. "You know we've had this dry spell for too many years and I'm taking a chance that it's heading in the other direction."

"I hope you're right." George reached for the screen door and held it for Ralph. "Go on in Ralph. I've got to head to the pump and wash. Annie would skin me alive if I went in with all this mud on me." He laughed.

Ralph laughed too and went on into the kitchen that was hot from the morning baking.

"Ralph Showalter! Come over here and sit down at the

table." Annie was a large woman and Ralph knew why. She was the best cook he'd ever known. Annie took a large pan of sweet sticky rolls out of the oven and put the pan down on a pot holder right in front of him on the table. Picking up a spatula she dug out not one roll but a plateful and shoved it his way.

"You still drink coffee don't you?" She had a twinkle in her eye.

"Yes'm." Ralph said as he picked up a roll and ate without hesitation. "That's about the best thing I've tasted since the last time I was up here."

He remembered that tasty meal Elizabeth Yates had prepared for them last week.

"How are the children, Ralph?" Annie asked.

"Fine," Ralph answered.

"Why didn't you bring little Lynn this time?" She sat down at the table with her own coffee and plate of rolls.

"Left him home with the girls. Nadine's leaving for Chillicothe tomorrow to go to school." Ralph told her.

"Has she got you eatin' yet?" George finally came in from washing up.

"You'd better get in here if you want any." Ralph told him.

"I'm coming." George came in and sat at the table. The stench from the hog pen clung to him, though it was apparent from his scrubbed face and hands that he'd made a good effort to rid himself of the barn lot mud.

Annie scooped out a third plate of rolls, poured more coffee and pulled another pan, hot and bubbling with brown sugar, our of the oven.

George crammed another roll into his own mouth. "Can't my Annie cook, Ralph?"

"She sure can." Ralph reached for his third.

They sat there eating and reminiscing for several minutes until George jumped up. "We got to get those hogs in the chute, Annie."

Ralph got to his feet and swigged the last of his coffee down.

"Come back in before you leave Ralph and I'll have a sandwich for you." Annie said.

"I will, Annie. Thank you. Those rolls would take first place at the fair." Ralph complimented her the best he could.

"They did." George told him and chuckled.

"You two git on out of my kitchen and let me get back to my baking." Annie shooed them through the back door.

Ralph and George headed for the barn lot where the hogs had been penned. Ralph jumped into his truck and backed it up closer to the chute.

"Back a little farther." George yelled above the squeals and snorts of the hogs. "Stop." He yelled again.

George threw a bail of straw into the truck bed then jumped in to spread it around.

Ralph cut the engine and jumped out of the cab of his truck and into the rear where he helped George scatter the straw down through the chute into the hog pen. Ralph joined George on the gate just above the crowded muddy pen filled with the familiar smell. George jumped into the mud while Ralph lifted the gate. They worked like long time partners, one guiding the hogs toward the chute and the other guiding them through the chute and into the truck. It took awhile to get the last hog in and they both ended up covered in muck and exhausted from the heat of the day. George began to close the gates of the chutes as Ralph secured the gate on the back of his truck. He'd never lost a load of hogs yet and he wasn't about to start today.

When the men finished, Ralph jumped down and the two of them headed towards the old pump to wash up. They worked at it quite awhile listening to the grunts and occasional squeals of their captives across the yard. Finally they grabbed the dipper and drank one after the other until they had satisfied their thirst. Then they just sat down on the grass in the shade to dry off and rest before each went off on their own again. They had done this before and it was always the same. Ralph appreciated the familiarity. There was a security in routine and sameness. That's what kept Ralph going.

Annie came out of the house with a plate full of sandwiches, a jug of milk, and a pie. This too was part of the ritual. Annie, like Bessie, would never have let them into her house smelling as they did, after wrestling with the hogs. She set down the tray and went over to the clothes line to check the laundry.

"Thanks, Annie." Ralph said as he shoved a sandwich into his mouth.

They sat quietly eating and drinking until most of the food was gone, watching Annie take the dry clothes off the line. They could match each other with conversation if they wanted but they could also be comfortable with silence, especially if that silence was accompanied by food.

"You got yourself a good woman, George." Ralph said.

"Yeah, you ought to get married again, Ralph." George wiped his mouth across the back of his hand.

"Well, I've been thinking about it." Ralph pushed his hat further back on his head. "I've been thinking about it." He repeated wearily.

"Are you a courtin' anybody special?" George inquired.

"No." Ralph said. "Just thinking about it."

George laughed and Ralph joined in.

"Well, I guess that's more'n you been a doing before." He smiled as he gazed across the lands that he'd been working from sun up to sun down for years just trying to keep a step ahead of the bank.

"I'd better be heading down the road." Ralph got to his feet and George followed.

They stuck out their hands to shake and George grabbed Ralph on the shoulder with his free hand. "Take care of yourself, Ralph."

"You too, George." Ralph turned and waved good-by to Annie who was headed back inside the house with a basket of clean clothes. She had a clothes pin in her mouth but she nodded her head briskly up and down and smiled, crinkling her eyes. He walked towards his truck, pulling off his hat and wiping his forehead with the sleeve on his shirt and then put his hat back on. George headed back toward the barn. There was always work to be done.

Ralph got to his truck and jumped in to turn the key and head off to St. Joseph. The engine sputtered, then hissed and steam came from the under the hood. He knew he'd better treat the motor with care or it would not get through the end of summer. The mechanics of an automobile engine were fairly simple but he did not enjoy working on one. His idea was to stay a step ahead of the problems by taking good care of what you had. His truck had lasted him a while and he intended to keep it going for a long time yet.

Ralph got out of his truck once again and found a bucket hanging on the pump handle. He worked the handle until the bucket was filled with water, then carried it back down toward the pig pens and poured it into the truck. He repeated this process until the radiator was filled. It was really low this time, Ralph thought to himself. He knew he should take it in to the garage and get it plugged. Maybe he could get it done before he took Nadine to Chillicothe on Thursday. He screwed the cap back on the radiator and pushed his hat back on his head. Wiping his shirt sleeve across his forehead he heard Annie yelling his name.

Chapter 9

When we arrived back at the farm, it was late. A storm was still brewing and lightning bounced beyond the few clouds that drifted above us. Small gusts of wind rustled the leaves of the dry crops adding an unsettled feel to an already strange night. The boys walked us to our place then went down to the barn to wash up at the pump and get to bed. Grabbing the bucket, we pumped water and spent the next few minutes carrying it to fill the tub inside and then locked the door.

"You go ahead." Cindy offered.

"Alright," I answered, thinking how different tonight was from that first night when we arrived so excited and scared of the unknown.

I took off my clothes and got into the water to wash. It felt good and I felt tired. I did not feel like talking and was glad Cindy did not pursue what we both knew Jack and I faced tomorrow. The farmer had made it very clear that anyone who got into a fight was out. Jack would be out of a job and I would not stay without him. I felt as though a heavy tarp weighed on me and I wondered how we would survive. I knew Jack always had a plan up his sleeve, but I never fully trusted his plans. I did know there was nothing I could do about it tonight, so I might as well enjoy the bath and the bed. Groping for my towel, I pulled myself up and out of the tub.

"Your turn," I tiredly told Cindy.

"Thank you." Cindy replied.

I put on my night clothes and lay on top of my bed staring at the ceiling and listening to the splashes Cindy made in the tub.

"Cindy?" I asked. "You don't think you and Cody

will have to leave too, do you?"

"I don't think so." Cindy said. "But Cody did tell me he picked up a flier about going to Omaha, Nebraska and working at the stock yards there. He said they were hiring and if the wages were good we might get a little place in town and I wouldn't have to do farm work. I could work in a shop or a hospital or something. I think when we get tired of this, or the work ends, that's what we'll do. Maybe you and Jack should head west too."

"I'll tell Jack about it tomorrow." I thought that sounded good to me except for the fact that it meant going farther away from Star City.

Cindy dressed, turned out the lantern and climbed into her bed. We heard another group of men coming in from town and wondered if Dirk was among them.

"We did lock the door, didn't we?" I asked for reassurance.

"Yes." Cindy answered.

"I guess we'd better get to sleep. Tomorrow is Sunday and you have the day off, but Jack and I may be afoot." I thought about walking long distances in the heat. It wouldn't be any worse than working in it except we'd get no pay.

"Goodnight." Cindy said sleepily.

"Goodnight." I echoed quietly.

I lay in my bed thinking of everything and nothing. My mind would not calm down and relax. I was angry, scared and sad all at the same time. The present situation was just something I could not comprehend. I lay unsleeping a long time and the night had grown quiet with only the occasional drift of soft voices from the direction of the barn where the men slept.

"Johnnie Belle?" Cindy asked.

"Yes." I answered.

"Will you always remember me?"

"Yes." I said. "I'll always remember you as my first grown up friend."

"I like that, Johnnie Belle." Cindy sounded like she was smiling. "I'll remember you the same."

I knew that we both would miss the relationship that had been growing between us. Laying quietly Johnnie Belle thought about that. Mama had always said that all we really had was the present moment. There were no promises of more and none could be relived. Thinking of Mama, I gave myself up to sleep.

Sunday morning had already arrived by the time Cindy and I awoke. The sun was streaming through the cracks in the walls and we could hear men talking. We both got up and dressed quickly wondering what the day would hold. When Cindy and I had made the beds and picked up our things, we opened the door and walked towards the outhouse. We saw Cody and Jack sitting under a tree chewing on grass.

"Go on Johnnie Belle. I'll go over and talk to Cody." Cindy walked toward the boys.

"Ok." I said as I continued walking slowly squinting at the brightness of the sun in my eyes. Knocking on the door and waiting a few seconds, I decided it was safe to go on in. I took a breath and dove inside as quickly as I could, wondering how people who didn't hold their breath stood it. It didn't take me long before I was back out in the fresh morning air. I walked over to where Jack and Cindy and Cody were.

"I'll be right back." Cindy said as she took her turn with the morning routine.

"Hi." I stood there wanting to know if Jack had talked to the farm owner but afraid to ask. By the look on Jack's face, I knew he could read my mind.

"He said we could stay over until tomorrow morning so we'd have a better chance of getting a ride to wherever we wanted to go. Dirk never came back last night." Jack said leaning back against the tree and looking at me.

"Where are we going to go?" I asked wondering what Jack was thinking.

"Thought we'd head down to Kansas City," Jack said. "Some of the men said the railroads are hiring down there. Sounds like something I'd like to try."

"What will I do? Where will we stay?" I asked desperately.

"Johnnie Belle, we'll find a rooming house and you can get a job in the city somewhere. There's lots of jobs in a city." Jack sounded confident. Once again, I hoped he knew what he was talking about. I sat down to think about this. I'd really liked the country. I'd never envisioned there could be so much farmland for one family and I liked the way you could see forever here in Iowa. But maybe I'd like the city too. I was dwelling on the idea of living in a big city when Cindy returned.

"Let's go eat breakfast." She said.

We all got up then and walked to the kitchen door to stand in the line. There was a hot breeze out of the south and I was glad for a day to organize my things and my thoughts before moving on. It could have been a lot worse I thought. Jack could have been hurt when he fought Dirk. I could have been really hurt too I suddenly realized. I was glad that Jack was there and glad he had protected me even though it meant we lost our jobs. I was grateful for Jack and not angry with him.

Breakfast was biscuits and gravy and bacon. We ate our share and then cleared our plates. The four of us wandered back outside to the tree and sat under its shade. It was nice to move slowly. We'd been told that we could ride into town on the back of the wagon and attend church with the farmer and his wife later that morning, but none of us wanted to go back into town that day. Lying under the tree seemed a nice way to spend the morning to me. Some of the men joined us on the gritty lawn finding places on the sparse pieces of dry grass. We listened to the talk of the men of different places they'd been to work. Some of them told what they knew about Kansas City and the railroad jobs they'd heard about there. Others told about hitching rides to other farms and finding jobs here and there. The more I listened, the less I worried. I wondered if they were saying things that they knew would calm our worries about leaving tomorrow, because it was certainly no secret, or if they really had experienced such positive adventures. The only thing I knew for sure was that these men were seasoned workers and they had the stories to tell.

After awhile, I decided to go to our shed and gather my things together and try to figure out how I'd be able to carry what I had while walking. Cindy and Cody took off together and Jack lay sleeping in the shade of the tree.

Inside the room that had been mine for only a short week, I took stock of my belongings. I decided to get rid of the torn dress and to roll up my things inside my bedroll. Maybe I could fix the bedroll across my back and tie it on with the rags that held it together. Not owning very much was a blessing in this circumstance. Wrestling with different ways to tie up my blanket I grew weary with it and put it down on the bed. I opened the slats on the window and leaned against the wood sides. The breeze was dry and hot but better than no breeze at all. I looked at the crops growing and watched as they waved like water as the wind blew through the field. The sky was a pale blue and off in the distance I could see that line of trees where the river was supposed to be. I wondered if there was any water in it. I wondered how any river could have water when it hadn't rained for so long.

I stood at that window for a long time soaking up the

landscape that seemed so foreign to me. I liked the quiet of this farm and being away from other people. Finally, I walked away from the window and sat on my bed. I pulled out the newspaper that had been given to me on the way up and decided to read it. It didn't take me long since most of it was small town news of no real interest to me. I lay back against the blanket that I'd mangled and fell asleep.

I woke sweating and hearing the snort of horses outside the window. I got up to look out and saw the team that pulled the wagons was there still hitched up and left at a watering tank. I watched them paw at the ground with their large hooves and shake their manes to rid themselves of flies. I could smell their sweat as they stood patiently waiting for their master. After awhile a couple of the men guided the team down to the big barn I assumed to unharness them and put them out to graze. I went outside and walked around the house to the swing I'd seen earlier. I sat in it and enjoyed the cool shade from the only other tree on the place. Eventually the dinner bell rang and I got up hoping to see Jack or Cindy and Cody. I walked towards the kitchen. Before I rounded the corner of the house I heard Jack's whistle. I turned and looked and saw him running across the yard. Waiting, I noticed that he seemed to be taller than ever.

"Jack Veazey, you get bigger everyday. Mama won't know you when you go home again." I smiled wondering just when we would go home again or if we'd ever go home again.

"Johnnie Belle, maybe you'd better look at yourself in a mirror if you think I'm the only one growing up." Jack said seriously. "You are becoming a beautiful young woman."

She felt herself turning red from his compliment always embarrassed when attention was called to her body, though she figured he was just trying to make up for the stress of the past days.

"You are too, Johnnie." He repeated what he said knowing she did not take him seriously.

"Let's go eat. Have you seen Cody and Cindy?" She just wanted to change the subject.

"No, but they won't be far now that they've heard the dinner bell." Jack laughed.

They got into the line and looked around. They saw Cindy and Cody coming from the girls shed and waved and left the line to meet them.

"Hello." Cindy called out.

"Hi." Johnnie Belle said with a smile.

"Ready to eat?" Jack asked.

"Sure are." Cody said and they all walked back to the line together.

Sunday dinner was served in the middle of the afternoon. Anyone who wanted to eat again had to go into town. Since there was no work on Sunday, though, most of the workers didn't feel the need to eat again. The afternoon passed quickly with talk under the trees, naps and games. Johnnie Belle enjoyed listening and watching it all.

Later that evening, the girls once again headed to bed and left the boys to themselves. Johnnie felt like she was sitting on the edge of a great canyon that was both exciting and horrifying. Laying in the dark that night, sleep would not come. Uneasiness moved from her chest to her stomach and back again. When she did manage to fall asleep, she jerked awake, feeling like she was falling from a great height and unable to catch herself. Restless, she got up and walked to the window and looked once more across the expanse of farmland under a moonlit sky. The sorghum leaves glistened white as they shimmered in the little bit of breeze. The dog lay against the shed slapping his tail in rhythm of some tune that was in his mind only, while the frogs croaked along. An owl hooted from a far off perch. Somewhere under that same sky was Star City and real family, she thought. Johnnie Belle stood there for a long time. She was more ready for this next trip than she had been for the first one. Experience counts, she thought. She looked out into the night. The vastness of the night made her think about God. Mama took them to the Baptist Church every Sunday and she used to pray every night before she went to sleep. She decided this was a good time to start that up again.

Johnnie Belle closed her eyes. "God, I really hope you know what you're doing with me and where we're going next, and in case it makes any difference, I want you to know that I like this farm country a lot. I know that you see everything, and I do trust you, but tomorrow I've got to go with Jack and I'm not so sure I trust the choices he makes. I'm going to miss Cindy and Cody. Lord, someday, maybe, if you could let me find a man like Cody who would treat me real special, I think I'd like to get married and have babies. Just keep your eye on us, if you would. I'm counting on that."

She opened her eyes and for awhile watched a lone cloud float across the stars.

Finally she went back to her bed and lay on top of the cover relaxing some. In her mind, though, she continued to see the fields of grain gently moving beneath the night sky, back and forth, silently. She was not aware of when, but she did fall asleep.

A rooster crowed.

Opening her eyes, Johnnie Belle lay trying to decide if it was part of a dream.

It wasn't.

Cindy jumped out of bed as though she too had been heavily asleep.

"It's Monday." I said sleepily.

We both got up. I went to fill the bucket; we washed, dressed and made our ritual trip to the outhouse. Coming back into the shed we straightened our beds. I put the extra bedding away and tied up my clothes like I'd worked out. Then I carried the bag outside and put it under the tree. Jack was already there.

"Hi." I said.

"Hi." He replied. "I got our pay. Are you ready?"

"I will be after we eat." I said. "I guess we get to eat."

"Yeah," Jack said. "The old man's been pretty good about the whole thing. But rules are rules."

Cindy and Cody came up and I studied them one last time.

"Let's go eat so we can be on our way." I said.

We all turned and walked to the door, made our way through the line. Breakfast was fairly quiet. No one discussed our leaving. We finished and were back outside again when the farm owner came over and told us he was headed to town if we wanted a lift.

"Thanks." Jack said. "We're ready."

We picked up our packs, strapped them on our backs and got into the back of his truck. Cody and Cindy waved. None of us trusted our voices and the break came swiftly and completely. We waved back and watched each other until the wagon went over the rise and then we watched the billows of dust. Jack and I remained quiet the whole trip to town. When the farmer parked, we jumped out and said our thanks and took off down the road toward Clarinda, where we would pick up a road south to Kansas City. It wasn't far to Clarinda, but most of the traffic seemed to be headed west towards Shenandoah. We walked.

Our jars of water were heavy but neither of us complained.

After about an hour a wagon pulled by mules stopped.

"Hop on!" The farmer hollered at us without looking.

Jack and I didn't hesitate. We threw our sacks in and jumped into the wagon. The rutted road bumped the old wagon until I wondered how it could hold together at all. About two miles down the road the old man turned off on a smaller lane. We grabbed our things and hopped off, the man never looking back at us. Jack and I watched a minute as he continued on his way, thinking we'd wave our thanks but to no avail. We looked at each other and laughed. We pulled out a jar and drank some of the water we'd brought then headed on. It was still early so the day hadn't gotten unbearable yet, but we knew it would be that way soon. We walked the better part of an hour when a car came up behind us and pulled over.

"Want a ride?" A man asked. "I'm going just this side of Clarinda."

His car looked barely big enough for us to fit into, but we climbed in quickly, crushing our few possessions to make enough room. I was jammed right up next to the man.

'Thank you for stopping." Jack said across me and the pile I was holding.

"Where you headed?" The man asked, leaning forward to talk to Jack.

"Kansas City." Jack told him.

"Where've you been?" He looked up at us in the mirror that hung down from the ceiling of the car.

"We've been working over near Shenandoah on a farm." Jack replied.

"Both of you?" They were talking as though completely ignorant that I was sitting between them.

"Yes." Jack said, and then added. "We come from Arkansas originally."

"Oh." The man said looking at us. "You two married?"

"No." Jack continued. "We're brother and sister."

"Oh." The man kept glancing at the mirror to look at us.

"You live around here?" Jack started questioning the man.

"No, just doing some business. I live over in Nebraska. Got to settle up some accounts over this-a-way."

I just stared out the window at the scenery flying by, uncomfortably hot and embarrassed to be so close to this stranger. I tried to concentrate on the land. It still amazed me at how far a person could see without a tree or a hill getting in the way.

"Your sister doesn't talk much does she?" He looked directly at me and I turned my head to look back at him then down, feeling myself turn red.

"She's a little quiet." Jack said looking at me and smiling.

I was almost wishing this ride was over when the man pulled off the highway and went down another smaller road.

"Maybe we should get out here." Jack said.

"No. You'll have less distance if you take this smaller road down here. It's not the main one but it's just a couple of miles shorter to town that way. I go that way when I'm around here."

"Well thanks, Mister." Jack said.

I wondered if he knew what he was talking about but it was too late because he pulled over suddenly and shut off the engine, the car making a noise like the shot of a gun. I jumped.

"Sorry sister." The man laughed. "Just a little backfire. This is where you'll have to get out if you're going into Clarinda. Just follow this road here up that ways. "I'm headed this other way."

I looked at him but didn't smile, then jumped out of the car right behind Jack. The man cranked it back up and it backfired once more.

"Thanks Mister." Jack yelled as the man drove off leaving us to stand in his dust.

I threw my sack over my shoulder and took off up the road, shaking my head and huffing at Jack.

"Johnnie Belle, slow down." Jack said running to catch up. "What's the matter with you?"

"That man." It was all I could say. "I didn't like him at all." I strode ahead with more energy than I had when we started out.

Jack caught up and we trudged on down the road, both of us hoping the man knew what he was talking about with this being a short cut, and not leaving us high and dry. The sun had climbed higher and the breeze had stifled somewhat. We stopped under a small tree at the side of the road and drank the last of our water and ate some biscuits the farmer's wife had wrapped up for us to take. We'd have to stop at a place soon and get more water in our jars.

Jack stood up. "You about ready?"

I stood up, pulled on my pack and followed Jack up the road. We came up a rise and saw a line of trees that probably followed a small river or creek bed. Beyond that we saw a farm house with some barns and decided we'd make it there and ask to fill up our water jars. We headed out to find work and a place to stay. Coming down the hill, we found the creek-bed nearly dry but the cool of the trees was refreshing and we stopped to rest again before the final leg into town.

Knowing the distance to getting water was short we slowed our pace somewhat and took in our surroundings. I did not know how long we'd been on the road but I was growing hungry. We approached the farmstead. There were a couple of big barns and some smaller sheds. A few cattle were grazing near a fence and we smelled a hog pen. The house was in need of paint which was not a priority with most folks these days. The yard was mostly weeds and a dog lay in the dirt under a tree near the front porch. The two story farmhouse held a wide porch with several steps up to the front door. The curtains hanging in the windows made the home appear soft and friendly. Reaching the steps, we moved up them slowly, stepping across the broken boards, then walked up to the screen door and looked at each other. The smell of food engulfed us and our faces held a look of hope. I glanced back down the road where we'd just been. The distant scene of the tree lined ditch, the road snaking its way across the rolling hillside, and the cattle nosing through the fence was peaceful. I liked this country. It was different than the country around Star City. In that peaceful moment I was glad I had come with Jack. I looked back around at Jack just as he reached up to knock on the door. I silently prayed that somebody would be home and that it would be a kind woman like Mama.

Chapter 10

Annie carried her laundry into the living room and dumped it out on the couch. She began to sort through it making piles. One pile was ironing that would have to be dampened down. Other piles would have to be folded and put away. It was one of those never ending tasks that moved Annie through her week. She could have done it in her sleep. She thought about Ralph and Bessie having seven children and she and George unable to have any. She shook her head thinking about Bessie dying right after the last baby was born. Such a shame, Annie thought. She stopped and looked out the big window that faced the road that ran in front of their old farm house and saw what looked to be two people walking down the road toward their farm. She could see far since their farm sloped down toward the river and the tree-line and she stood watching the two small figures move slowly on the road in the dust and heat. They seemed to be carrying a load of something. Annie picked up a towel and folded it up, placing it into the stack on the couch. It was unusual for people to be a walking down their road from that direction, especially with the heat of the day coming on. Sometimes they saw people on the road driving from Shenandoah. It was a short cut to town, but those who lived beyond them were pretty far out for going on foot.

The pair ambled slowly. Annie thought they were probably looking for work. They had a lot of that kinds in the area in the past years. She hoped they weren't looking for work from them because they could barely keep themselves going. The drought had sucked the life out of their farm and their bank account.

Annie watched until they finally got close enough to see that one was a woman, maybe a girl, and the other a man. She saw them stop and look toward her house. Probably trying to decide if they should stop and ask for work.

Annie felt saddened. She hated to turn away people in need. At least she could offer them some water, food and rest for a moment. She worked quickly to fold up the bundle of laundry that was sprawled everywhere by now and put it quickly away. When she got back to the living room to gaze out the window, she saw that they carried a bundle each. She watched them turn slowly into the driveway that edged the house on that side and walk questioningly up the dirt path. The girl looked to be about 16 and the boy not much older. Probably a young couple starting out on their own, she thought. She went into the kitchen and set out some plates and glasses on the table. Glancing out the kitchen window she noticed Ralph had pulled his truck hood up and had walked to the pump, and grabbed a bucket to fill with water. She wondered if he was having trouble with his truck or just needed a little water.

Just as Annie moved back towards the living room she heard the knock on the screen door. She surveyed them carefully as she moved through the room and towards the screen noticing a new hole in the wire across the door. She'd have to remind George to fix that. Not having money to keep the place up was hard, but she would not leave an open invitation for flies to come into her house.

Her attention turned to the young couple. They were both thin and browned from being in the sun. She thought the girl reminded her of herself when she was younger. Smiling sadly she tried to remember when it was that she lost her own figure and blossomed into the woman she was today. It had actually happened gradually over years of cooking for neighboring farm crews that helped during harvesting. That and church dinners. Annie remembered the box of clothes in the attic that she still saved from those early days after her marriage to George. Times had been better then. She thought she should get that box down and give some of those clothes away. Why, she could give a dress or two to this girl and maybe Ralph's girls could surely use some. Why hadn't she thought of it before now? Maybe she'd holler at Ralph to hold up while she got out the box. It would be easy to get at, she knew because, she often crept up to the attic and knelt beside it dreaming of days gone by.

"Hello there." She said in a motherly tone, opening the door. "Won't you two come in for some cold water?"

The two looked at her and the welcome they were receiving and then looked at each other both wondering if they were dreaming. They had hoped to get a drink from the well, and to maybe rest under a tree, but this woman was inviting them directly into her home.

"Come in. Come in." She said again standing back. "I saw you coming from way down the road. We don't get too many people walking from that direction. Where are you from?" Annie was curious about these two. They were young enough that she could be their mother. Everybody had a story, she'd learned from the years. Some were happy stories and some were sad. Most were a mixture of the two. Annie ushered them into the kitchen both amazed at how she seemed to just accept them as they were, dirty and hungry. She told them to wash up, pointed to the wash basin on the kitchen cabinet, and then hurried out the back door. They looked at each other and began to wash neither one speaking a word. It felt a little bit like being back home with Mama telling them what to do.

"Ralph." They heard her yell and looked out the window to see a man putting water in a truck engine.

Jack looked at Johnnie Belle, both thinking this must be her husband.

"Ralph, are you having trouble?" She asked.

"No, just need some water." Ralph said.

"Say, Ralph, I have some old dresses I want to send to your girls. Nadine might be able to wear some of them."

"Sure." Ralph said his head still under the hood looking over the engine.

"I'll get them from the attic. Come to the back door and holler at me when you're ready." She said.

Ralph knew that he would not get back inside of her house today. He laughed.

"I'll be there directly." He said as the pigs squealed at their captivity in this heat.

Annie hurried back into the house and found her two guests still standing there in the center of her kitchen.

"Well, sit down." She said and pointed towards the table. She pulled out some sandwich spread from her icebox and bread she'd baked that morning and told them to make themselves some sandwiches and she'd be right back. She set some milk out and went into the other room. They heard her going up some stairs.

The two still had not said a word. But no one had to tell them twice to eat. They sat and began to spread the meat on the bread and pour themselves some milk. They heard her upstairs. It sounded like she was dragging a box. They just continued to eat and drink and look at each other. They could hear her coming noisily back down some stairs. Pretty soon she came in the doorway from the living room dragging a box.

"Ma'am, do you need some help?" Jack asked as he jumped up from his chair.

"No. No. I've got it. You just sit down and eat up there. Well, now what a dusty place that attic is, and hot." Annie turned around, dusting herself off and fanning herself. She began to go through old clothes in the box and pulled out dresses, one after the other. Then she went to the back porch and got an old flour sack and put some of the dresses in it. "Ralph!" She yelled.

"Coming," The man answered. Johnnie Belle and Jack

glanced at each other and watched him through the open kitchen window as he turned and headed toward the back door.

"Now, take these things to your girls, Ralph." We heard her say.

"Thanks Annie." The man took the sack and walked back tossing it into his truck. "Got to get these pigs to St. Joe Annie. Be seeing you."

The woman had followed him out. "Wait 'til I get you another sticky bun to eat on the road. Then I've got a young couple in the kitchen that might need a ride to town. They came down the road from the west. Young and hungry and probably looking for work."

Johnnie Belle looked across the table at Jack, both of them hearing every word of the conversation just outside the window.

Ralph slammed the hood down on his truck. "You can tell them I'm headed for St. Joseph. They can ride along as far as they want.

"One's a woman. Probably his wife." Annie said.

"Well, tell them if they want a lift, I'm due to get down the road." Ralph got another drink from the well. He wasn't one for standing around and he'd already wasted good daylight.

It wasn't a minute more when Annie burst back into the house, sweat drenching her thin dress.

"Thank you, ma'am, for the food and milk. It was right nice of you to go to all this trouble but we best be gittin on down the road." Jack stood up. "Unless you got any work for us here."

Annie could hear the southern accent and figured he was from Oklahoma.

"There's a man out back who is headed south to St. Joseph" Annie added. "He said he'd give you a ride and he might have some work for you, himself."

"Can we trust him?" The boy asked.

"Trust him?" She seemed shocked. "Why he's the most honest man you'll ever run across, young feller." Annie pointed her finger at Jack. "He's raising seven kids and all alone at that, since his wife died a few years ago. Annie couldn't imagine anybody questioning the reputation of Ralph Showalter. But then again, these kids didn't know him from the devil, and from the wary looks on their faces, she thought, maybe they'd met that devil somewhere along their way.

They looked at each other and Jack nodded. "Sure. We'll take the ride."

Annie wrapped up some food for the three of them in a bundle and heard the screen door on the back porch open. She looked out to see if it was Ralph or George coming back from the barn. It was Ralph. He looked at her impatiently. "Annie, I'm ready to head out if those two want to ride with me." Ralph stayed outside of the door not even stepping inside the porch to get into the shade. He knew by now his smell would have developed to a worse degree than before.

Jack and Johnnie Belle stood up and followed Annie out onto the porch to meet their latest traveling companion. The smell of a barnyard too long in the heat filled their heads. Annie handed the wrapped food to the man just beyond the open door, then stood back and held the door for them to go out.

"Oh, wait just one more minute." Annie bustled back inside and returned with a bundle of clothes. "I think you might be able to wear these." Annie sounded out of breath and was fanning herself again. She handed the clothes to the girl.

Johnnie Belle looked down at the dresses and then looked Annie in the eye gratefully, but hesitated.

"Go on, now. Take them. I can't wear them anymore and never will." She looked down at herself then looked back at the girl with a wistful expression.

"Thank you." Johnnie Bell reached out and took the dresses, unable to fully express to this woman her feelings for the kindness she had shown them in the short time since they'd first stepped foot on her porch. Annie smiled and the girl smiled back, then looked down and followed the boy out the back door where the man was impatiently waiting.

The man came over and put out his hand to Jack. "Ralph Showalter"

"Jack Veazey. This here's my sister, Johnnie Belle." Jack put his arm on my shoulder. "We're right glad to make your acquaintance and grateful for the ride." Jack turned around to the woman. "Thank you, ma'am. We appreciate all you done for us."

The woman smiled. Ralph was looking impatient to get on the road. He headed toward the truck, and the squeal of the hogs.

"Are you ready?" Showalter asked us but was already opening his door.

"Yep." Jack replied and pushed me into the truck ahead of him.

I climbed in thinking the smell inside this truck was worse than any outhouse I'd ever been in. This man appeared to have rolled in the stuff. At least she did not have to worry about the way she and Jack must smell. The truck lurched forward and the man waved to the woman who stood beside the clothes line with her hands on her hips.

"The missus said you was headed to St. Joe." Jack had to yell to be heard above the motor, the pigs, and the wind. "I was thinking about trying to get work on the railroad in Kansas City. Saw a sign about them hiring." I was content to sit back against the seat, gasping for fresh air and letting Jack talk.

"Well, I don't know about that." Ralph wondered if this young fella would be a hard worker. "Where you from?"

"Arkansas." Jack answered. "South of Pine Bluff. Star City."

"That right? I've been down there hauling fruit back up here. It's pretty country. What's your folks do?"

"Our Mama cleans houses and does the wash for people. Our Step-daddy ain't too good fer nothin'." Jack wasn't one to mince words.

Ralph considered this and figured at least the kid was honest enough. Nobody'd make that up.

"What kind of work you done?" Ralph went on.

"Well, I worked mostly in the cotton fields. Hard work, but all there is down there. Course, now it's dried up, and everybody's heading north or west." That's what's brought us up here. We hopped a truck up this far." Jack didn't want to go into the trouble they'd had back at that farm. He looked at Johnnie Belle. She glanced back at him.

Once again Ralph considered this information, chewing on a piece of clean straw.

"I could sure use a hand on a new piece of land I bought." Ralph pushed his hat back and scratched his head. The truck rumbled down the dirt road. Ralph was trying to make up for lost time.

Johnnie Belle listened to the conversation, bouncing roughly against the two men, glad she hadn't eaten more than she had. Ralph just kept his eye on the road ahead.

"Well sir, I think I might like to give it a try if there's a place for us to board real cheap. Is there work my sister could do?" Jack looked at me knowing I would probably not speak up at all.

Ralph thought for about that. He was always ready to help out. "I reckon I could use the extra help around the house and garden. My oldest girl is leaving for college soon and I suppose the others would be glad for the help since they'll be going back to school in September. Since my wife died, it's been hard on the girls. I've still got a young boy who needs lots of tending to."

I wondered what his children were like. This would certainly be different than the farm work. I began to feel anxious about getting into a situation that we knew nothing about. Of course, that farm woman had said he was a good man and she seemed awfully nice herself. I was a good housekeeper and certainly knew a little about taking care of little boys. It would be a chance to stay out in the country for awhile instead of living in the city. I'd like that. I took a deep breath trying to feel calm. Nobody asked me straight out if this was what I wanted. I guess Jack just figured I'd go wherever he went. He was right about that. No matter how anxious I felt, I was not about to take off on my on.

"You own much farmland?" Jack inquired.

"Not now. Farming hasn't been so good, but I picked up a few acres awhile ago and I think things will start to turn around here one day. I'm thinking it's time to move back into it. Mostly I truck produce between Iowa and Arkansas."

"I'm hoping to make some money up here and go back and get married." Jack explained. "Johnnie Belle's looking to start out on her own at something."

They were quiet for a long way each one of them alone with their own thoughts and memories.

"I'll tell you what we'll do." Ralph said. "If you two want to come back to my place, I can put you up and feed you in exchange for some pay and work. Some of my neighbors could use a part-time hand too." Ralph looked over at Jack.

"Sounds good to me. How about you Johnnie Belle?"

Jack looked at me.

I nodded though not enthusiastically, and looked at Jack trying to question him with my eyes to see if he felt certain about this.

"Alright then." Jack said. "We'll give it a try."

"We'll take this load of hogs to St. Joe. and get back home for a late supper." Ralph looked thoughtful as though figuring just how long it would take them, knowing he was already off his schedule and thinking about how long it would be until supper. Then he remembered the food Annie had sent and felt better.

"What part of the country are you from?" Jack asked.

"Actually I've got a place just southwest of here about 40 miles. But we've got a little trip ahead of us with these hogs." Ralph pushed his hat back on his head and seemed to settle in for the ride, and then spoke again. "Sorry I can't take time to drop you off at the house, but I've got to get to the stock yards in St. Joe before they close."

"We're just real glad to get the ride and work, mister," Jack said.

"Call me Ralph." He said.

Ralph pointed out of his window. "I was raised up that way about six miles and my Dad still owns the farm. My brother Davie and his wife Ruth and their family live over that way about three miles." Across that field over where the tree line is, near that river, is my house.

"The whole time he talked he waved his arm and pointed. It was as if Ralph Showalter knew everybody and all about the land that draped across the miles we traveled. From the sound of his voice and the description that he gave, he loved this farmland. I sat listening as he went on and on talking about the land and the people he knew who lived in the farmhouses we saw. His voice was calming and I nearly fell asleep.

We were in Missouri now but it was like Iowa except that it had a few more rolling hills. Jack asked questions about this crop or that farm and I enjoyed the trip even with the smell of the hogs. Finally, we came to St. Joe. Ralph seemed to know the streets. He drove to the stock yards and backed up to unload his truck. Jack jumped out to help. When that was done, he pulled the truck over to an office building and went in. When he came back out he had some papers that he crammed into his pocket. I watched him walk. He was tall and lean and strong looking. His hair was black, his eyes brown and his skin was tanned. He didn't seem rough like the men on the truck from Arkansas. When he got back into the truck he looked at me but didn't say anything.

Ralph started up the truck and wondered how long it had been since his girls had gone so long without talking.

"I've got 5 girls." Ralph directed this at Johnnie Belle. "Yes, I've got five girls who never stop talking. You'll be a nice change to have around."

"Five girls?" I asked surprised at the information and myself for spurting out the question.

"Well, one's heading for college later this week." Ralph could have told her that another one of his girls was staying right here in this town with their doctor, but he didn't want to explain that.

"I lost my wife several years ago and life's been hard, but we seem to be surviving." He drove the truck back through town seeming uncomfortably quiet after sharing that bit of personal information. He watched the road and drove steadily as though he could have done it in his sleep.

I was intrigued with this family that had so many children and no mother. I could not imagine not having Mama. But then I'd never experienced having a Daddy like this one appeared to be: a man who could talk about his children with love and take care for them without a wife. This man was different than any I knew. We traveled back north and into the land that was home to Ralph Showalter. He drove the dusty country roads too fast, racing the swirls of dust and heat that rose under the wheels. Before long he pulled in beside a house that stood next to a huge tree with a swing hanging from a limb hidden under it's leaves. The house was neatly painted white. There were at least two sheds. One looked clean like it had new paint. There were a few chickens pecking in the dry grass and a dog who did not stir from his cool spot under the porch.

"Well, here we are." Ralph seemed to say to himself as much as to us, and he jumped out of the truck almost before it stopped rolling. A young boy, stocky and as brown as the dirt ran out from the back of the house.

"Daddy." He cried.

Ralph grabbed him and swung him up on his hip then put him down and the young boy squirmed away.

"Mary made cookies today." The youngster told him all the time looking at the strangers with him. "Who are they?"

Getting out of the truck slowly, stiff from the trip, sweat clinging to their dirty bodies, Jack and Johnnie Belle stood quietly.

"This is Jack and Johnnie Belle Veazey." The man looked at us. "And this is Lynn. Now, let's go wash up for supper." Ralph walked toward the back of the house. He opened the screen door. Jack and I followed him into the porch where he hung his hat then sat down on an old chair.

"You two go on into the kitchen, I'll be there in a minute."

Jack pushed me ahead of him onto the linoleum floor and into the kitchen. Behind us, Ralph began to pull off his muddy farm boots, pushing the wooden door closed, and leaving us to stand their looking at each other.

The smell of beans caught my attention and I looked around. I saw a big kitchen table, a cook stove, and a wash basin on the kitchen cabinet. The table was set. I could hear a piano being played and a radio on. I glanced at Jack. He was doing his own survey of our surroundings.

"Dad." One of the girls yelled as she bounded into the room. Just at that moment Ralph, pulled the door back open and came in. He had changed from the mud covered clothes he had been wearing to others that were crumpled but cleaner.

"Darlene," he said. "This is Jack and Johnnie Belle Veazey. They are looking for work and we're going to put them up awhile. Show Johnnie Belle where she can put her stuff and I'll show Jack the shed. Then they can wash up for dinner. Mary, put on some extra plates.

Looking at Darlene, I could see I was a big surprise, but none-the-less she smiled.

"Come on." Darlene said and led me into the living room. "This is Mary." She said. Mary headed past us into the kitchen to set out more plates. "Betty's in on Daddy's bed playing dolls." Nadine's upstairs getting ready to leave for college tomorrow. We'll make you a bed on the floor till Nadine's gone; then you can sleep in her place."

"Thank you." I thought that Darlene seemed to enjoy being the one in charge here. I followed Darlene up the stairs to a big room with two big beds. I put my stuff down.

"Come on." Darlene was headed back down the stairs. I followed her back into the kitchen where she pulled out more silverware and told me to go to the porch and grab a chair, which I did. I saw Jack and Ralph coming back across the lawn, Lynn in tow.

"Let's eat." Darlene yelled at no one in particular as the men came in and the piano stopped playing. Betty came in and looked at me.

"Sit down." Ralph said and we all did.

"That's our Mother's place." Betty said to me.

"I'm sorry." I looked shocked and got up.

"Sit down." Ralph said to me. "She didn't mean you couldn't sit there. She was just remembering. We all do that from time to time." Of course he knew that most of Betty's memories came from stories the others told her. She was pretty young when her mother died to remember much of anything, Ralph thought.

"You talk funny." Betty said with a smile.

I was glad for the smile.

"That's because she must be from the south." Mary said.

"We are at that." Jack said smiling at the girls, flirting somewhat.

With that, talk went to Nadine's plans for her move to school. Beans were passed, bread was buttered and Nadine went to the sink to slice more tomatoes and cucumbers. I was grateful to be eating so I did not have to talk. The attention to our southern accent made me uncomfortable. As soon as we'd finished, Mary and Darlene got up to clear the table telling Nadine to stay seated since it was her last week at home. They brought cookies and got out an ice cream maker. The family moved outside under the tree in front of the house and churned until the sun tired out and sank beyond the tree line. Bowls were produced and we ate once more. The ice cream cooled us down and made it feel like a party. I smiled at Jack and he knew I was happy to be here. Ralph Showalter got out a mouth harp and played a little jig and Betty and Lynn danced around. I thought about Cindy and knew she would have enjoyed this family experience. I could see her and Cody having a family just as happy one day. It certainly was different than my family had been. The stars were coming out and bugs began to bite at us as if to declare ownership of the area. We ate until we could eat no more. Mary and Betty lay on the grass and gazed at the stars which were beginning to appear. I was tired, full, and happy. Pondering the events of the day, I felt overwhelmed with all that had happened. I took a deep breath and emptied my mind of everything but the pleasure of this night. I felt a gentle breeze and embraced the moment.

Chapter 11

"Girls!" Ralph called, his voice held authority. He knew they had stayed up late the last few nights and would be slow to move if he did not get them started. Besides the excitement with Nadine going off to college, the girls were getting to know Johnnie Belle Veazey. Ralph was the one to get things going in the mornings and his mind moved from the house to the farming, to his trucking. Lately he had been busy trying to finish the clearing of that new piece of land so they could get it plowed up before the winter and ready for the spring planting. Today he had to leave it to Jack and he hoped Ralph Wendell would be there to help. Seems that most of his days were spent in the Miller's garage in town working on cars.

There was a lot to be done before they took Nadine to Mrs. Baxter's. "Get up and get to the chores." He waited there at the bottom of the steps for a sound of some kind. He rarely went upstairs. No reason to. Ralph yelled again. "Nadine, you up?"

Nadine rolled over and aimed her voice down the stairs. "I'm awake." She slowly sat up in bed and then moved her feet onto the floor. A rooster crowed from the yard. She usually got up ready to meet the day but this morning she had the feeling that this day was different. She sat up. Today was her last day at home. Today was her first day as an adult, on her own.

Nadine had not felt like one of the kids since her mother died, knowing the younger ones looked to her for some guidance. The loss of her mother had stolen a part of her. Not that she blamed anybody for that; it was just the way things happened. Up until that day, Nadine had not fully understood the struggle a household had to make ends meet. She wasn't sure if she took it upon herself, if her Dad had needed her to do it, or if it was just one of those things that happened in life. Regardless, Nadine knew that her childhood had been cut short. Today it became official. She was an adult going out on her own. Part of her was sad, part of her scared, yet another part of her was excited. She wondered if she'd ever come back home.

"Get up Darlene." Nadine ordered. "You have to check for the eggs because I have to finish getting ready to go to Chillicothe. Mary, go out to the cellar and bring up a new jar of apple butter for breakfast."

"I hate getting the eggs. Mary, will you?" Darlene rolled over and looked at Mary who was still trying to open her eyes.

"No." Mary whined. "I hate those laying hens."

"Betty, you want to get the eggs?" Darlene tried again.

"No!" Betty yelled. "I hate chickens too."

"Girls? You up?" Ralph hollered once more. He had to let them know he was serious; that the day had to get under way.

"Yes." Nadine called back down understanding his meaning.

"I put the milk in the kitchen. Somebody skim it. I've got to walk out in the pasture and check that fence. Lynn's with me."

"Alright," Nadine said again. She got up and looked out the window, the breeze blowing her gown.

I got up off the pallet and folded up the blankets, watching the scene before me.

"Good morning!" Mary said. She stretched her arms up and out, accidentally hitting Darlene.

"Mary!" Darlene pleaded. The bed was pretty small

for three of them.

"Good morning." I said. I turned around and pulled my night gown off and hurriedly put a clean dress on. It was the last one I had brought with me. "When is wash day?" I asked the girls.

"Monday," Nadine said looking at Johnnie Belle's small bag. "But if you need to borrow something we can share. We share all the time anyway."

Suddenly I remembered the clothes the woman in Iowa had given to me. "Wait." I told them. "I have that other bag of clothes that Annie Grove gave to me. I'm sure she gave a sack to your daddy as well, for ya'll. They must still be crammed behind the seat of the truck."

Johnnie Belle saw the girls look at each other and was not sure what it was that she said.

Nadine thought it was funny hearing Johnnie Belle talk. And even though they called their father, Daddy, other people always referred to him as your father not your daddy.

"I'll go look on the back porch." Darlene jumped up excitedly and without changing from her nightgown dashed down the stairs with Betty chasing right behind. "Daddy might have tossed the sacks there."

Nadine smiled at me.

"Say that again, Johnnie Belle." Mary said.

"What?" I looked at her not understanding what she wanted me to say.

"Ya'll." Mary tried to draw out the southern accent.

"Leave her alone, Mary. If you went down south, you'd sound just as different." Nadine told her pointedly hoping that Mary had not embarrassed their guest.

I knew that Mary didn't mean anything by what she said, nor did Nadine, but I also knew I was different from them and wondered how I would fit in around here. I busied myself with making the bed and folding up my own clothes.

"We found them." They both heard the girls yelling as they came dragging the sacks filled with dresses up the stairs.

Nadine and I helped dump them out on the bed. We spread a few out and held them up to get a good look. They were a little old fashioned but well made and would make serviceable housedresses.

"I want the flowered one." Darlene held up a shift to herself, swirled around and pulled it over her head. It looked way too big for her but I kept quiet.

"Wait." Nadine looked at me. "Which ones did she give to you, Johnnie Belle?"

"It doesn't matter." I said, glad they were as thrilled as she had been to get the clothes. "Let's just share them all. Except, Nadine, you should pick the best ones to take with you to school."

"But that's not fair." Darlene looked hurt.

"Keep the flowered one, Darlene." Nadine told her. "I'll pick something else."

Darlene swirled around them and grabbed another one. "Here, Mary, try this on." Darlene held out a blue checked one that Johnnie Belle thought was so pretty.

Mary did as told and whirled around. She could not remember ever getting clothes like this before. After their mother died, Daddy had tried to get them to remake some of her clothes, but they just didn't fit at all and besides they seemed to them to be old lady dresses.

"You two better go and get your chores done before Daddy gets back." Nadine said sternly. Both girls went down the stairs, followed by Betty, who didn't seem as interested in the clothes and had pulled on the same dress I'd seen her in yesterday, and we heard the back screen slam.

"What should I do?" I asked her.

"You can set the cornbread on the table and skim the milk if you want." Nadine began to fold up the dresses.

Johnnie Belle helped her.

After working in the hot fields, Johnnie Belle was glad for a chance to do housework again. She noticed Nadine picking up one of the dresses admiring it.

"This one's torn." She said mostly to herself. "Maybe I can figure out how to use Mama's old machine and fix it." Nadine mused to herself.

"I'll go start breakfast and then maybe I can help you with that machine. My mama has one and she taught me some how to sew."

Nadine listened to this girl who sounded so different from them. "We'll work on it after breakfast." She paused, and then looked back at Johnnie Belle. "Thank you."

I went on down to the kitchen and heard the dog bark. Looking out the window, I could see Darlene coming back with her flowered dress pulled up in front and full of eggs. Maybe that dress a few sizes too big worked for her. Mary slammed the screen door and put the jar of apple butter on the counter. Then she stuck some wood into the stove and scooped last nights ashes from the bucket back into the stove. It smoked and she shut the door.

"I'll get the water on." She said as she carried the ash bucket back outside and headed toward the cistern. "Betty come with me." She hollered out as they left.

I set the table and cut the bread. Then I looked through the cabinet until I found something to put the skimmed milk in. Darlene came into the kitchen with the eggs and put them into a pan.

"We'd better cook some of these up for breakfast." Darlene said as she got a large skillet out and plopped some grease in. Then she set the skillet on the stove and stood watching it slowly melt the lard.

Nadine walked in. "What are you doing?" She went towards the stove where Darlene was waiting for the grease to get hot.

"I'm going to fry up some eggs for breakfast." Darlene said, trying to sound grown up.

Nadine raised her eyebrows as though surprised at Darlene's helpful attitude.

"You just sit down, Nadine. Johnnie Belle and I can handle this." Darlene put on one of their mother's old aprons and wiped her hands on it.

"How can I help?" I asked Darlene.

"You can crack those eggs for me if you want."

Nadine smiled knowing that Darlene always got shells in the eggs when she cracked them. "Why don't you fry enough to make some egg sandwiches for the trip to Chillicothe?"

"We will." Darlene replied.

Mary came banging in the door, sloshing water from the bucket. I went to help her out. Though I wasn't a whole lot bigger than either Darlene or Mary, I was strong. I lifted the bucket and poured the water into the large dishpan on the stove. Mary went and dipped some of the water out into the wash basin and carried it back to the wash stand.

"If you want to wash your face, the rags are under here." Mary showed Johnnie Belle the cabinet door under the wash basin where there were towels as well.

"What should we do with the cream?" Johnnie Belle asked. They had never had a milk cow, but her cousins had and she had skimmed milk at their house.

"Put it in the butter churn and give it to Betty to put in

the cellar. If we were going to be home today, we'd use it for baking." Nadine stared out the window.

"Are you excited about going to school?" I asked her.

She looked back at me smiling. "Well, yes and no. I can't say it won't be nice to get away from the kids, but then, I'll miss them too, I suppose. I really miss our mother."

Darlene looked at me and I looked over at Nadine. I was not sure if I should reply or not. I had a feeling their mother's death wasn't talked about much.

"I'm sorry." I said.

"Thank you." Nadine looked at me. "Here comes Daddy."

Betty ran out the back door to meet them and almost collided with Lynn.

"Wash up." Ralph hollered at Lynn.

Lynn came bounding in with Betty right behind him until he saw me. Then he stopped. Ralph came in and Lynn slid between his legs toward the wash basin. I smiled at him. Harold wasn't that much younger than I was, so it had been a long time since I had experienced having a little boy around. He made me smile. They washed then went to the table where Mary was pouring milk in the glasses I had set out.

"Let's have some of those eggs, Darlene." Ralph had heaped bread on his plate. "Just put them on top of the bread."

I went over to get his plate from the table.

"Thank you, Johnnie Belle." He said. "Are the girls showing you around?"

"Yes." I said meekly, glancing his way.

Jack came in then for breakfast. "Morning, everybody." Jack nodded, washed up and sat down. I could see he'd already been helping Ralph with chores.

"After you finish that field, Smith is going to need you for a week or so if you're willing." Ralph looked up to see if Jack would agree to the work.

"Yes sir. Thank you, Ralph. I appreciate all the work I can get."

Darlene was dishing up the eggs onto the bread and breaking most of the yolks. I delivered the plate back to Ralph.

"Thank you." Darlene looked at Nadine with questioning eyes. They had seldom heard their father be so formal.

Ralph began to sop up his eggs with bread that had been spread with a heaping amount of apple butter. Lynn watched him then began to do the same. Finally, all the eggs were done, the sandwiches made, and Darlene and I sat down between Mary and Nadine.

"Are you ready to go?" Ralph asked Nadine.

"Yes." She answered. "My stuff is still upstairs."

"Soon as you're finished breakfast, go and bring it down."

"I'll help you." I volunteered. They all looked at me, but I was sure it was not because of what I said. It was because of the way I talked. I felt myself blushing and looked down into my plate.

"Thanks." Nadine said.

"You girls going to go with us today, or stay home and bake?" Ralph looked at Darlene.

"We're going with you." Mary said.

Darlene hated long car trips, often getting sick, but she was not about to miss seeing where Nadine would live and go to school this next year. She had lost her mother and now she felt as though she was losing her sister. Even though Nadine was bossy, she knew she'd miss her. Nadine reminded her of their mother. "I'm going too." She said.

"Johnnie Belle you can go with us or stay here." Ralph got up and headed out the back door.

She had looked around enough to know that the house was pretty dirty and could use a good cleaning, but she wanted to go. She was beginning to feel that she was a part of this family. "I'll go if there's room." She remembered traveling in the small cab of the old truck.

"There'll be room enough." Ralph said as he let the screen door slam and then yelled back through the door. "You girls get the dishes cleaned up, Nadine bring your things down and I'll load the car. Lynn, feed the chickens."

We all quickly finished scraping our eggs off our plates and scooping them into our mouths. We downed bread and milk and gathered the dirty dishes to the dishpan. Nadine ran upstairs and back down into the kitchen with the dress I had promised to help her with.

"Johnnie Belle, let the girls finish those dishes. Will you help me with this?" I followed her into the living room where she grabbed some mending that was heaped over the treadle machine and put it aside.

"Sure." I replied following on her heels. I lifted the lid and pulled the heavy head of the machine up into position. It looked almost like Mama's. After wiping the dust from the machine, I picked up the dress and knew exactly what needed to be done. We found some thread and prepared the needle. I pulled out the chair and began to restitch the torn dart in the back.

We heard the younger girls in the kitchen washing and drying the plates and forks and glasses, then putting them back into the cabinet.

"Betty wipe off the table." We could hear Mary ordering. "I'll sweep the floor." Lynn was in the yard calling out to the chickens. Nadine ran back upstairs and brought the rest of her things down packed to go. We were all rushing, trying to be ready when Ralph called us to go. I had been there long enough to know that when he said he was ready to go, he had one foot in the car and was ready that instant.

"It sews just like my mama's." I said thankfully.

Ralph came into the house and through the living room. "What are you girls doing?" He asked.

"Johnnie Belle's helping me to stitch up this dress Annie Grove gave us." Nadine held up the seam I had sewn.

"Well now, that's good of you Johnnie Belle. Maybe you can get those other girls to sew." Ralph pushed his hat back on his head. "We'd better get going."

Ralph picked up Nadine's bags and walked back through the kitchen towards the car. We heard him slam the trunk down and yell, "Let's go!" Finished, I handed the dress to Nadine and she folded it up to carry with her.

Mary and Darlene dropped their dish towels over the kitchen chairs and ran out the back door. Betty dropped the broom where she had been standing and followed. Nadine picked up the broom and stood it in the corner. She looked at me and shook her head as we followed. Everybody hopped into the big old black car, Betty bickering with Mary about who would sit where. I wasn't sure if the rush out was to vie for seats or if it was because Ralph was an impatient man. I had a feeling it was a little of both.

"Wait!" Darlene jumped out of the car and headed back into the house. Coming back out, she had the bundle of egg sandwiches that she'd wrapped in a tea towel in her hands. Crawling back into the auto she gasped, "I almost forgot lunch." She slammed the door.

The car pulled away from the house with the sounds of bickering between the younger three children, dust flying through the windows and bodies squished together. I thought about Ralph Showalter. I knew he worked hard and loved his children. It was obvious he needed someone to clean the house and I thought I could be happy doing just that. The girls seemed easy enough to work with. Of course there was Lynn. He didn't seem to take to me just yet.

The ride was much smoother than the one in the old truck had been. I enjoyed the speed and the wind that whipped my hair. I wondered what Mama and Harold were doing today. I thought about Sister and hoped she was happy with Bobby. It seemed an eternity since I'd seen them. I wondered about the rest of my life, but only for a moment. It was hard to think beyond the moment in the current closeness with so many others. Leaning back against the seat of the automobile I closed my eyes and remembered life before leaving Star City. I'd been so happy with the repetition of daily events there. Sometimes it seemed as though there would never be such normalcy again. Opening my eyes I watched the fields race past, farm homes shaded by big trees, and a few other cars and trucks out in the sticky heat. I felt content. Maybe, even happy. For now that was all that mattered.

Chapter 12

The cadence of farm life kept Ralph moving forward. Mornings always arrived on schedule, just as the sun set each day with regularity. He managed to keep up with the trucking, farm a little and tend to his children fairly well. Though according to Aunt Ruth he was spoiling Lynn and he needed a wife. The garden produced, the food got cooked, clothes were washed and dried and sometimes ironed, bread baked, mending done, and church attended. Since Johnnie Belle had been there, though, he had to admit things were running smoother than before, everything that is except his relationship with his sisters.

As he drove through the tiny town of Craig, Ralph pulled the car up to the only store, which just happened to be owned by his sister Emma's husband, Loren. He had a list of things to get but he dreaded seeing Emma at the counter when he went in. She always was one to speak her mind.

And, as if on cue, the minute he walked through the screen door, Emma started in. "Ralph, people are talking. You keeping that pretty young girl up to your house and then even taking her to church!" Emma jumped right on him before he could wipe the sweat off his brow. Couldn't she move on to another topic? Wasn't there anything else going on in Craig? If people were talking it was because she fueled the flames.

"Emma, just get me that salt and sugar and mind your own business." Ralph was used to Emma. She'd fussed at him for getting married young, and then for starting out on his own with the trucking business and not going directly into farming. Farming was a hard life and a poor one at that. Ralph like doing business, he liked to drive and he'd found a way to make a fair living doing just that. Though it had taken a toll on him lately, those government loans made it a whole lot easier to get a farm and Ralph needed to take advantage of it. He hoped he knew what he was doing, and he liked his life just fine. Emma never liked farm life either. Couldn't wait to get married to a business man and move into town in a little house with nothing more to tend than a couple of children and her flowers.

"Ralphie, if you needed help with the house, you could have asked me."

"Emma, leave Ralph alone. He's not going to take advantage of a young girl. Give your brother some credit." Loren shook his head and walked over close to Ralph.

"Sorry, Ralph." he said. "You know how it is. Those women at church let their tongues wag more than what they should."

Ralph had not anticipated this problem when he let Johnnie Belle and her brother come to his place. Maybe he didn't figure they'd stay this long. Maybe he didn't fully understand the mind of the local women about such things. He thought his own sisters would understand, but apparently they did not. So, he just ignored them all. Jack was a good worker and since Nadine left, Johnnie Belle had made the house shine like it hadn't since Bessie had been alive and, besides that, the girls took to her. Darlene had taken up sewing and Mary was learning to bake. Maybe he hadn't thought it through initially, about the gossip, but that's because he had nothing to be ashamed of. He had always helped people out. People always think the worst even when they know you, he thought.

"Emma, why don't you and Loren come out tonight and visit," Ralph smiled. Emma might just like Johnnie Belle if she'd give her half a chance.

"We're going out to Dad's farm." Emma spit out her words. "You haven't visited him much since he remarried."

Emma had him there. Dad remarrying after all these

years and Muriel being quite a bit younger than him had been hard to accept. Talk about a stir. But it had upset Ralph more than he liked to admit. He wasn't sure why but he was having trouble accepting a stepmother who was not a whole lot older than himself. Maybe if he'd seen it coming.

"I'm a busy man, Emma." Ralph picked up his purchases and headed for the door. "Loren." Ralph tipped his head. "Be seeing you Emma."

Ralph pulled off hoping to get home without getting another flat tire. He was too tired to fix one today. It was Saturday night and he was going to take a bath and catch Edgar Bergen and Charlie McCarthy or Benny Goodman on the radio.

The wind blew through the truck window carrying with it the dirt from the road and coating the sweat on his skin. It was just a short drive home but he was impatient to get there because it was so hot. As Ralph pulled up in front of the house and parked under the shade of the tree, he saw Johnnie Bell in the back at the edge of the yard, in the garden weeding out the old vegetation. The coolness of the shade calmed him as he got out and stood there hoping the scant breeze would dry the sweat running down his body. Summer did not seem to be giving in to fall easily this year. September was just a few days away but the heat would not subside.

The garden never looked better he thought, even with most of the summer vegetables dried up. There were some fall vines still managing to thrive among the tilled soil. He watched her move. He smiled inside at himself. Was it the garden that looked good or the gardener? She was small even for her age, but pretty as a flower. What if Emma was right? Johnnie Belle was certainly a different kind of woman than he'd known. He enjoyed her soft southern accent and had noticed the way she gently laughed. On the long drives he found himself thinking about her. She waved at him now. He waved back then stood by the car pretending to gather up some papers in the seat, but really considering the strangeness of his feelings. He shook his head at his thoughts. It was Emma's talking to him. It was the heat. He headed inside.

Johnnie Belle seemed to take life more seriously than they did or maybe it was just that she was so quiet? She didn't talk about her up-bringing much except that she'd had a step-father that she seemed indifferent towards. Often she spoke of her "Mama" as she called her and her brother and sister, so he knew that she missed them.

Maybe Emma and Ruth were right about him. What was he thinking when he brought this young girl here. But she needed work and had really helped out with the girls and the house, and of course the garden and he could honestly say he had no ulterior motives at the time. He was too easy with his own girls and Johnnie was taking up the slack. He probably should just make his girls mind better, but Ralph had never been a good disciplinarian, so how was he to begin now?

Johnnie came across the lawn with a large basket of small squash. Ralph met her and took the basket.

"Thank you." Johnnie looked at him and then back at the garden. The pumpkins are blooming." Johnnie was a small girl with hazel eyes, brown hair, and tanned skin. "In Arkansas we fry the blossoms." She smiled at him knowing he would not make fun of her about it. She had actually overcome her shyness with him and enjoyed his company.

"In Arkansas they fry everything." Ralph said smiling, trying not to look into her almond shaped hazel eyes. He found himself breathing deeply.

Johnnie's short hair had begun to grow out and she pulled it back into a bun at the nape of her neck. He wondered at himself noticing things about her. That wasn't like him at all.

"I like to come out here early in the mornings and later in the evenings," she said. "We ate supper already. We didn't know if you'd be back." She smiled again.

"That was good. Where's Lynn?"

"He's inside with the girls listening to the radio. We already hauled water and took baths. The tub is all yours now." Her drawl was soft and melodic to Ralph's ears. He stood there looking at her, glad he had not been around when she took her bath. That would have been awkward. Somehow, Johnnie Belle sensed things like that and was able to work around the times he was gone from the house. Though Ralph always let the girls bathe first so the water would be cleaner. It didn't much matter to him if the water was a little dirty. The bath situation on Saturdays had already been worked out. Darlene told her that since Bessie died, their Dad always managed to be out of the house Saturdays after supper so the girls could take their baths in the kitchen in the old metal tub. He'd get home later and take his while they listened to the radio in the living room or sat out front enjoying the evening.

"Johnnie Belle," Ralph turned toward the house with the basket of squash, and Johnnie Belle followed. "I want you to know that I appreciate all you do here. You've been good for the kids."

He kept his eyes on the basket of squash and continued walking. He did not look at her. She could not tell if he was just thanking her or if he was trying to tell her something else. For a talker, he did not always communicate well. Was he was trying to tell her something else? Jack was leaving next week to go back to Arkansas. Maybe Ralph was tired of her being around and suggesting that she should go with him. His words could be a dismissal of a sort. The feeling made her feel sad and lonely. They walked on toward the house not talking.

She stopped at the back door. "I'm going out front to watch the stars come out." She walked on around the house with the dog at her heels.

That's where Ralph found her after he was clean and had put on some fresh clothes. They sat on the stoop together watching the stars, listening to the radio through the screen, but hearing Betty and Lynn argue about something.

Ralph looked over at Johnnie Belle. He felt stirred at the sight of her sitting there in the moonlight. She was beautiful. He winced at what Emma would say.

"Johnnie Belle, did Jack come by today and tell you he's going back to Arkansas?"

"Yes." Her heart sank as she looked at him wondering if he was going to suggest that she might want to go back with him. She'd come to love this place and the Showalter family. The girls were like sisters to her, and though Lynn never let up, challenging her at every turn, she had grown to love him. She respected Ralph and sometimes felt deeper feelings inside of her, yet too afraid to face them. Maybe she *should* go back with Jack. She was almost afraid to ask but decided it was better to know. He was awfully quiet about something.

"Do you want me to leave with him?"

"What?" Ralph looked at her wondering if she was tired of all the work here. What if she was homesick and was ready to go on? He had not thought about her leaving being such a jerk on his emotions.

"Would you like me to go too?"

"Go where?" Ralph looked at her wondering if this was her way of telling him she was tired of all the work around this place. He would not really be surprised. Who would like having to take the helm of a house with so many children and so much work to keep up with? He was suddenly saddened about the prospect of her not being around.

"Wherever I was going when I came here, I guess. To St. Joe to get work, or Kansas City. I could always go back home with Jack." Johnnie Belle thought about that. She really was content here and would like to stay, but she realized that she was really just an after thought when he hired Jack. He was probably ready to get his life back to the way it was before she came. Johnnie Belle figured that maybe she was in the way. Then of course there was the talk between the women at church. No one had said anything to her, but she sensed that they thought the situation was inappropriate and their looks did little to hide what they thought.

Ralph thought for a moment trying to decide how to answer. If she wanted to leave, then he needed to let her go. Maybe she wanted to go but was afraid he could not manage without her. Could his recent feelings mask the fact that she was tired of keeping house and tending his kids? He never was very good at seeing things like that and there was no secret that his dealings with women went lacking.

"No. I mean, not unless you just *want* to go." He knew from the way she always talked that she missed her family, or maybe she was ready to leave and do something else. After all, what was here for her? What would happen to her if he did get married to somebody one of these days?

"Well, I would like to see Mama, but I really love this farm and the girls and Lynn." And, I like you a lot too, she thought, but did not say it out loud. Their shoulders touched as they sat close and Johnnie Belle felt the thrill of physical contact with this man. She was afraid to look at him.

"I'd like you to stay, Johnnie Belle." Ralph said softly, feeling their physical closeness and finding it was almost unbearable holding back the response he really felt.

She looked over at him and for a moment, they made eye contact. But it was long enough for her to understand that there were feelings between them. She looked away. The front screen door flew open and Lynn and Betty came out.

"McCarthy's over." Betty said.

Lynn crawled onto Ralph and Johnnie Belle moved over to make room for him. Betty sat down between them and leaned on her. Johnnie put her arm around her small shoulders hugging her.

"I'm sleepy, Daddy." Lynn yawned.

"That's because it's bedtime." Ralph picked him up and carried him into the house to the bedroom that they had shared since he was a baby. Johnnie Belle rose, taking Betty's hand and went in as well. They all headed for bed knowing that Sunday mornings were hectic with everybody trying to get ready for church. Ralph came back out of his bedroom just as Johnnie Belle was ready to follow Darlene, Mary, and Betty up the stairs.

"Goodnight Girls." He called. "Goodnight Johnnie Belle."

"Goodnight Daddy." They called back to him.

Johnnie Belle turned around and looked right into Ralph's eyes. This time they held their gaze.

"Goodnight Ralph." She said, and then ascended the stairs.

Chapter 13

Ralph noticed that Johnnie Belle was an early riser. Since Bessie died, he'd had the early mornings all to himself. Now when he got up, however, Johnnie Belle would be out in the garden, tilling the soil or tending the late fall crop. He watched her carry water from the cistern, work blisters on her hands, and pick the grasshoppers off the plants. In the beginning, he would watch her from the kitchen window, enjoying the way she moved. Her small frame was unlike Bessie's. Her brown hair was just barely long enough to be pulled back off her face. Ralph noted that she was a hard worker and had not complained once. She was good at settling arguments between the girls too. Things had been a lot calmer since Johnnie Belle had come. This morning he decided to go out and join her in the garden. He was drawn to the calmness of the task of weeding, the coolness of the hour, as well as to the company. He knew there would be little conversation, but that suited him for now.

"Morning." Ralph spoke quietly, hoping not to waken the girls. Their window was open and faced this side of the yard and Ralph had a voice that would carry across a field if needed. Johnnie Belle replied without looking up. Of course she'd heard the screen door when he came out so she was not startled by his greeting. She continued squatting; pulling the ever persistent weeds, old vines and stirring up the leaves that had begun to drop off the trees. Her movements were even and sure. He squatted where he stood and began to work beside her. Neither spoke. He looked up at her once and caught her glancing back at him and he smiled. She smiled back. It was an innocent look, but the feelings that were exchanged in that brief moment caught him off guard. There in the garden, Ralph became more aware of his attraction for her. The strength of his feelings took him by surprise. He wondered when he quit seeing her as Jack's sister who helped around the house and began to see her as a beautiful young woman that he was definitely attracted to. He was glad she had decided to stay on longer than Jack but he wondered if it would be temporary.

Ralph soon realized the day was getting ahead of him and shaking himself free from his emotions, he stood up.

"I've got to holler at the girls to get up and head into the field."

Johnnie Belle looked up at him and smiled in reply. His heart lurched. He pushed his hat back on his head and turned to go.

"I'll see you when you get back." She spoke with that sweet drawl that southerners have, stretching a one syllable word into two.

Ralph glanced back over his shoulder and smiled but kept walking. His step was just a little bouncier than it had been for a long time. He went to the window and yelled up at the girls. Going into the kitchen, he grabbed a towel filled it full of biscuits and some ham and headed out for the day. His mind, however, remained in the garden with Johnnie Belle.

Johnnie watched Ralph's truck roll down the road. She stood up and stretched her back. There was work to be done. She threw some of the weeds into a pile over the fence for the milk cow and picked up the bucket filled with what was the last of the squash and headed for the house. Darlene was sewing a new dress for school and Mary and Betty both needed one as well. She had caught up on the mending and was teaching Betty and Mary the skill. She needed to put up some of the squash for winter and Mary promised to help her. Mary was organized in the kitchen and Johnnie Belle was glad to work with her. Going into the house she put the squash on the table and Lynn came in from the bedroom.

"Where's Daddy?" He pouted.

"He had to go do some field work. He'll be back this afternoon." Johnnie Bell was too busy to pay much attention to him.

The girls came in moving slowly and washed up.

"Johnnie Belle, will you help me braid my hair?" Betty asked.

"Sure, Betty, sit down over here." Johnnie Belle took the comb and tried to rake it through Betty's thick and wavy hair. Her own was straight and fine. She wished for hair like this.

"Betty, let's go to the pond." Lynn knew he was not allowed there without his father.

"Daddy said not to go to the pond without a grown up" Betty told him.

"We can go if we want to." Lynn said back at her.

"Lynn," Darlene came in. "You can't go and you know it. If Daddy caught you, you'd probably get a spanking."

Johnnie Belle finished Betty's hair and went back to cleaning vegetables. Mary got a knife and began to pare off the stems of the squash while Johnnie got water on the stove to cook them down. They heard Darlene humming as she sewed. Betty ran out the front door and Lynn sat pouting at the table.

By noon, the canning was about finished and Johnnie Belle and Mary decided to wait until after they ate to haul the new produce to the cellar. They both sat down and fixed some leftover beans and cornbread and poured milk from the bucket. Betty came in and finally Darlene.

"Where's Lynn?" Betty asked.

We all looked at each other and jumped up at the same time. Betty began yelling his name, but the rest of us didn't bother. We ran out the back door and crawled over the fence in the direction of the pond. Lynn was not very good at minding any of them when Ralph was gone so it wasn't difficult to guess where he was.

They ran breathlessly over the hill and across the pasture. They could see him standing at the side of the nearly dried up pond, in the mud, poking a stick at some frogs.

"Lynn!" Darlene called. "You get to the house right this minute!"

"Lynn!" Mary yelled. "Daddy told you not to come down here!"

"Lynn!" Betty ran to him. "What's that?"

I just stood there with my hands on my hips wondering if Lynn would ever mind when Daddy was away. Funny, I thought to myself, about calling Ralph, Daddy. Around here that was his name so it was hard to think of him as Ralph.

It felt good to be out of the house and there was a breeze. "Since we're all here and most of the work is done, why don't we just stay awhile and let him play." The girls all looked at me with surprise.

"Yeah" Lynn squealed.

"Me too?" Betty cried.

"Sure." Darlene looked at me and we both lay down on the grass and enjoyed the breeze coming off the small section of water. Mary and Betty and Lynn threw clods of dirt.

After awhile, Lynn came over and sat beside me on the ground.

"I'm sorry, that I didn't mind." He looked down.

"It's alright, Lynn. We were just worried that you'd drown." Johnnie Belle told him.

"I think we'd better get back home now." Johnnie Belle looked at Darlene to see if she agreed.

Darlene got up and took off up the hill to the fence.

"I'll race you." She yelled.

We all took off after her, but I held Lynn's hand to keep him from stumbling into all the holes and ruts, and to assure him I wasn't mad. We caught up with the girls at the cistern, washing the dirt off. A car pulled into the drive.

Lynn and Betty recognized it as Aunt Ruth and Uncle Davey's car and ran to it immediately. The rest of us followed.

We greeted them and invited them into the kitchen where we got water to drink. For a man, Uncle Davey had a soft voice where Aunt Ruth's was husky but not loud. They sat at the table with us. I was always uncomfortable with Ralph's family. I felt like they did not approve of me for some reason.

"Well, Johnnie, how are you getting along here?" Uncle Davey asked kindly.

"Fine," was all I could manage to say and I knew I blushed even through my sun browned skin.

"Ralph's not working you too hard, is he?" Aunt Ruth asked.

"No." I told her. She asked kindly as though she really cared.

"We brought a cake." She said as she put a tin on the table. "Thought you might like to share it?" I had heard about Aunt Ruth's cake baking skills but had never tasted one that she'd actually made. We had her recipes though, and the girls had used them a couple of times since I'd been there.

"Can we eat it now, Aunt Ruth?" Lynn asked, squirming up into her lap.

"Well, have you been a good boy?" Uncle Davey asked, teasing.

Lynn looked at each of us afraid of what we would say. We all looked at him smiling.

"Mostly," he said, but bowed his chin.

"I guess that's good enough for a rough little boy like you." Uncle Davey replied.

Lynn smiled and so did the rest of us. We all wanted to eat the cake. Darlene got up and got some plates and forks and a knife to cut it. She handed the knife to Aunt Ruth.

Aunt Ruth proceeded to cut and serve. "How long are you staying here, Johnnie Belle?" She asked.

Shocked at such a direct question, Johnnie Belle looked up at her. "Why, I don't know, ma'am. I guess I haven't decided yet." Johnnie Belle knew that most people around this place seldom used the word ma'am, but it was so ingrained that Johnnie found it hard *not* to use.

"Well, we heard your brother left and went back to Arkansas awhile back." Uncle Davey spoke frankly.

"Yes, he did." I replied. "He's getting married."

"He is?" Aunt Ruth looked surprised. "Well now isn't that something. Was it a local girl?

"Oh no," Johnnie Belle told her. "He's been engaged since we left Star City. He came up here to earn some money so they could afford to get a place of their own."

"Do you have similar plans?" Aunt Ruth persisted.

"Oh, no ma'am," I answered her quickly and almost choked on the cake.

When I recovered I continued. "I like it here. I thought I'd stay as long as I'm needed." I was startled to hear myself being so forthright.

All of our heads turned as Ralph's truck pulled into the drive next to Uncle Davey's car. Johnnie Belle wished he'd slow down before he got close to the house. His speed always seemed to raise the dust more than necessary and it eventually found its way into the house.

"Hey Davey, Ruth" Ralph called through the window on his way to the back door.

"Hello Ralph," they both called as he entered.

"Daddy, Aunt Ruth brought her cake. I've been good so I got to eat some." Lynn was covering all the bases.

Ralph grabbed a plate and a chair and Ruth cut his piece while Ralph looked at me with a raised eyebrow.

I knew why. He'd sensed they came to check things out. I even understood why. It wasn't proper for a young woman to be staying in the home of an unmarried man. There were times that I was uncomfortable with it, but only since I knew that I had feelings for Ralph that were more than hired help is supposed to have. When Ralph and me and the kids were at home everything seemed fine and perfect. At church or when we went to town, there were looks and talk. I had told Ralph I shouldn't go out with them as a family as it wasn't right, but he insisted. He was a stubborn man.

Ralph took a breath between bites. "What's up Davey?"

"We heard Jack went back south and thought Johnnie Belle might have gone with him, so we came over to see if the girls needed some help."

Ralph looked at them with a slight smile. "No." He said lazily. "Johnnie Belle's going to stay for awhile and help us out. Why, she has really kept this place together, especially with Nadine gone."

I could not look at anyone. I just stared at my hands in my lap feeling embarrassed, wondering if my feelings, or his, showed.

"Girls, I want you all to take Lynn fishing down to the pond." Ralph told them.

We all looked at each other and smiled.

Lynn's eyes got big and round but just as suddenly he jumped off of Aunt Ruth and shouted. "Let's go." He grabbed my hand. "Come on Johnnie Belle." I had become his ally.

We all took off out the back door trying to keep up with Lynn and laughing at the whole situation.

"See you later." Ralph hollered at us.

"Bye, Daddy!" The girls yelled.

We all strolled across the grass and climbed back over the fence. We ran and played and enjoyed the breeze, full of cake and with a sense of freedom. After awhile we heard Uncle Davey and Aunt Ruth start up their car and leave. Directly we heard Ralph's truck backfire and figured he'd gone off again. Johnnie Belle sat down in the grass and relaxed wondering where he was going now. She had fallen in love with this little farm family, maybe more than she was willing to acknowledge. Laying herself out on the dry and pokey stubbles of grass, she watched some birds building a nest in a nearby tree and wondered why her life couldn't be as simple as theirs.

Chapter 14

"I've got a load to haul to Arkansas on Thursday." Ralph said. "Would you like to go and visit your family, Johnnie Belle?"

Supper was about over and the girls were clearing up. Lynn grabbed a jacket and ran out to swing. The nights were getting shorter and cooler and it wouldn't be long before this activity ceased until spring. It had been a couple of weeks since the visit from Aunt Ruth and Uncle Davey and Ralph had not been the same. I sensed that something was bothering him and I was afraid he had decided that it would be best for me to leave. Neither of us had brought up the subject of the supposedly inappropriate situation I created by being in the household. Nor had either one of us given any verbal confirmation of the relationship we both knew was forming between us.

Johnnie Belle looked at him. Ralph said he wanted her to stay with them and she had, knowing that this was what she wanted to do with her life. She thrived on his small farm, around the girls, and little Lynn. But more than that, she thought she was falling in love with Ralph Abraham Showalter. Since that morning in the garden, she'd seen a change in how he looked at her. She knew that he saw her as more than just one of the girls. He saw her as a woman. She felt it, until that day they got the visit from Uncle Davey. Did they say something to change his mind? Maybe Ralph was just being nice to her and she had it all wrong about his feelings. But just because he asked if she wanted to go to Arkansas on a run, did not mean he didn't want her there at the farm. Maybe this would be a chance for them to spend some time together without the others around. She could find out what her feelings were all about. It was a chance to see Mama and Harold. She'd like that.

Johnnie Belle thought for a moment. She wondered if he really had to go to Arkansas or if he was doing it for her. She did not care. She shoved the confusion away and smiled.

"Yes!" She finally replied. "I do want to go. How long will we stay?" She carried some dishes to the dish pan then returned to the table, looking at him but seeing Star City and Mama in her mind.

"I've got to pick up some apples on Friday and get them back up here before they spoil, so it would be just a couple of days."

"Oh." Johnnie Belle felt disappointed, but still glad.

Ralph saw her face drop. "I'll have to make several runs down there over the month. You can stay down there and come back on one of the other trips or go and come back with me each time. Or if you decide you don't want to come back," Ralph paused and looked away, "Well then, I guess we'll deal with that too." Ralph thought that maybe she was ready to go back and stay. Whatever he did he wanted her to be happy. She was young and he wanted her to be sure about her choices. He worried that the excitement he'd felt between them was one sided. Eventually he'd find out. If she didn't want to come back, he'd know alright. He hoped he was right about her feeling something for him because she stirred up emotions he thought were gone forever.

Johnnie Belle looked up at him and smiled, excitedly. She missed Mama and Harold. She could hardly contain herself to finish up the dishes. She turned on the stove to heat water. Darlene wiped the table and Mary began to sweep the floor.

"Can I go, Daddy?" Betty asked.

"You've got to go to school." Ralph answered her. She ran outside to play with Lynn. They were used to Ralph's trips but Johnnie could tell, he wasn't happy about leaving the girls and Lynn. He never was. She hoped the weather changed this year so the farming improved. If the farming improved, he could be home more, but he did what he had to do for now. Johnnie Belle did realize that everything he did was part of an unwritten plan he kept in his head. His sharp mind had figured out a way to make a living farming and it involved trucking until it all came together. At times he would share bits and pieces of the things he dreamed about and Johnnie Belle treasured these moments.

They finished the dishes and the girls worked on school work. Johnnie picked up a book Darlene had brought home and read some in it. Finally she put it down. She could not concentrate so she went out front to sit on the stoop and think about Star City once again. She would not think about her relationship with Ralph until she was back home with mama once again.

When Thursday arrived, Aunt Ruth came out early before the children were out of bed for school so when Johnnie Belle and Ralph left, it was only her at the door waving good-bye to them. She could tell Aunt Ruth was not pleased with this situation of the two of them traveling together and Johnnie Belle knew she was only willing to help because she hoped that Johnnie Belle would not return with Ralph.

Johnnie Belle had put a change of clothes in her tote sack and threw it in the floor of the truck beside her feet. Ralph just threw a clean shirt on the seat between them, and a small bag that contained his razor and comb. He started the motor and backed onto the dirt road, turning south toward their destination. The trip was long and hot. They did not either one talk much but there was a pleasant feeling of being alone together. Johnnie Belle thought it was probably the first time since her arrival, almost four months before, that they'd been alone, together for any length of time. Ralph brought water in a jar and she had wrapped some bread with butter and some ham up in a towel, so when they got hungry they could just eat and keep driving. The only stops were at for gas and

Ralph always checked the water in the engine and the air in the tires. In the heat of the afternoon, we had a flat. Ralph jumped out to fix it as he had done many times before.

Our conversation was light, but when our eyes met, they communicated something deeper, intended or not. Both of us were well aware that there was an emotional pull between us yet neither of us was ready to discuss it. I wondered how long we would go until it came up. For now, though, he was still Ralph Showalter, the man who hired Jack and me, and I was just Johnnie Belle, the girl who helped in his home. For now that was okay with me. I was finding it difficult to deal with the excitement of going home again. I did not know how to deal with the conflicts love was bringing about. It was more complicated than I had imagined. Maybe Ralph was feeling the same way, or maybe he wasn't. He had so many things to deal with that romance was probably not important to him right now. I decided that I was in no hurry and was glad that apparently neither was he.

"Johnnie Belle, we're here." Ralph touched my arm lightly and shook me awake.

I looked up, wiped the sweat from my face and looked around. Star City. I smiled, more excited than I'd ever been in my life. Ralph handed me the jar of water we'd refilled at the last stop and I drank.

"Which way?" He asked me.

"Go down that street right there." I pointed. "Then turn down there." I pointed again. He followed my direction as he drove slowly. I was sitting on the edge of the old and worn truck seat and memories came flooding back. The town looked smaller and more depressed than I remembered it, but I was happy to be here.

"There." I pointed. "That's my house." It looked tired. The yard had no grass, it needed paint, and there was Mr. Jim's old truck with the hood up and two flat tires.

I felt like I'd been gone years. I felt old. When I left I remember feeling small and young and afraid. What had happened to me? A lot, I told myself.

Ralph pulled up in front of the house under the shade of an old tree and shut off the motor. We both opened the doors, glad to get out and hoping for a breeze. The front door opened and Harold came running out.

"Johnnie Belle!" He yelled hugging me. I hugged him back. I never thought I'd be so glad to see Harold.

"I missed you." He said. "Mama's at the Prather's."

"Good. We'll walk up there." I told him. Then I turned and looked at Ralph.

"This is my brother, Harold." I said. "And this, Harold is Ralph Showalter."

"Glad to meet you, Harold." Ralph reached out and shook Harold's hand.

"Glad to meet you." Harold replied.

Ralph knew that Johnnie had posted letters to her mother from time to time and they knew who he was.

"Johnnie Belle, I'll pick you up on Saturday morning, right here, if you want to come back." Ralph looked at her trying to make her understand that he wanted her to do what was best for her and she certainly did have a choice. He figured he needed to know how homesick she was and if she really preferred living on a farm in Missouri to her own home in Star City. He hoped she chose to return.

Johnnie Belle looked at Ralph, startled. She had every intention of going back to Missouri. She loved it there. Was Ralph trying to tell her something? She held his look for a few moments trying to decide what he meant. Did he want her to go back with him? Was she wrong thinking that he was as attracted to her? She didn't know what to say, so said nothing. Ralph got back into his truck and waved as he drove down the street, slowly so as not to stir up any more dust than he had to.

Johnnie Belle stared after him until Harold grabbed her arm. "Come on." He said, and she turned forgetting Ralph for the time. They headed off for the Prather's house where Mama was working late.

As they approached the house, Mama was coming out the back door.

"Mama," I cried out.

Mama turned around and looked at me with surprise.

"Johnnie Belle, why didn't you write you were comin' home," she hurried over to us and hugged me.

"I didn't know." I told her. "Ralph had to come down to Arkansas for a load of apples so he asked me if I wanted to come down and see you."

Mama pushed her hair back out of her face and pulled me close.

"Let me look at you." She smiled and shook her head.

"You look to be five years older and ten years prettier." Mama looked proud.

"Jack and Mary Jacobs have set a wedding date for December." Mama went on.

"Are you here to stay, or will you be going back to Missouri?"

"I'm going back." I said with some uncertainty, knowing what I wanted but unsure if it would happen.

"How long are you here? Come over here and sit down." Mama drug me over to some chairs that were set beneath a tree.

"Ralph said he'd be here to pick me up Saturday morning."

"That's not long enough, but I'm glad you're here. We

miss you Johnnie Belle."

"Luther Draper broke his arm jumpin' from that tree at the swimmin' hole." Harold said. "That big old branch just broke right off."

"That right?" I ruffled his hair. At 14 he was part boy and part man.

It was nice. We sat and visited like we never did when I was home. Then Harold and I went to walk around town and told Mama we'd meet her back at the house. Harold told me that Mr. Jim hadn't changed any over the summer.

"So how about you?" I asked.

"I got a job, Johnnie." Harold said excitedly.

"What kind?" I was surprised.

"I'm helping some men repair the Baptist Church. Don't pay much but I like it and I'm learning a skill, Mama said." Harold pulled himself up tall.

I looked at him, his dark eyes and freckles shining out in the soft twilight. He was growing up too. I hoped it would be easier on him than it had been on me. We ended up at the grocer and I bought Harold a root beer.

"Are you going back up to that place in Missouri with that man?" Harold asked me as we sauntered home.

"Yes." I answered him.

"Why?" Harold asked me.

"I like it there. I like his family and the work I do." My mind could see us all as we sat out front of the house eating home-made ice cream. "Mama was right when she said there's no future for me here in Star City."

"You didn't have to settle so far away, did you?" Harold looked at me. I felt bad that I had left him.

"Jack's back. He and Mary will settle here and you'll

have him close by."

Harold was quiet for awhile.

"Do you help Mama with me gone?"

"Sure do."

"Let's go home and bake some cookies." I suggested.

"Too hot," Harold laughed. "Want to die of heat?"

"Well, you're right." I laughed trying to think of something to get his mind off my leaving on Saturday. "How about making some ice tea?"

"That I'll help with," Harold seemed happier and we walked up toward the front of the house.

Mr. Jim was there on the porch.

"Hello, there Johnnie Belle. When did you get back to town?" He hollered but his voice was small and raspy.

"Today. I'm going back to Missouri Saturday morning." Harold and I walked past him into the house. I could not bring myself to hug him.

I enjoyed being home and missed it more than I knew. That night we all sat out on the porch to be cool. We watched the moon rise and the stars flicker on, one by one. It was late but we didn't care and it was like old times. Later, I lay in bed thinking seriously about staying in Star City. I fell asleep content and comfortable about my life.

On Friday, Harold went to work with the construction crew and I went with Mama. I told Mama about Ralph and his family and how his wife had died leaving him with the children. I told her about the land and the garden and how much I liked living in the country. Mama watched me and listened. I could see in her eyes that she was happy to see me so happy. As I talked about Ralph, his work, how gentle and kind he seemed to be, respected in the community, and enjoyable to be around, Mama just kept listening and watching me. I guess she'd never heard me go on like that before. . .

That next night as I got ready for bed, Mama came into my room and sat down. She picked up my doll, straightened its dress and put it back down.

"Mama," I said. "I can't decide if I want to go back with Ralph tomorrow or stay here. I've missed you so much and I'm so happy here."

"Johnnie Belle, did you hear any of what you told me today?" Mama did not wait for me to answer. "You're happy here only because of what you have found by leaving here. Your path has taken you to Ralph and I think your heart belongs with him too. Here, you're content, but your life should be more than that.

I looked at Mama. I had always been content in Star City because I hadn't known anything else. But now I did know about something else. I knew about love. And I knew I loved Ralph Showalter, his family, and his way of life.

"I miss him, Mama." I said.

"I understand, Johnnie Belle." Mama pulled the cover back and I crawled on top of the sheet, clammy from the humid air.

I sighed. "I'll miss you and Harold."

"I know." Mama kissed me on the forehead and left my room. As I lay alone in the dark, my feeling of contentment faded and an unsettled feeling overwhelmed me. I was facing my own feelings and needs instead of giving in to what was comfortable. I wanted to go back to Missouri. I wanted to be part of the Showalter family. I thought I wanted to be Ralph Showalter's wife.

I gasped. There alone in my own room, in my own bed and I was shocked at myself. His wife? Was I really ready to even think about marriage? I lay for a long time wondering about who I had become. How could I have changed so much in such a short amount of time? I wondered how he really felt about me. I did know that it was time we discussed it. Would I have the nerve if he didn't bring it up?

I fell asleep and dreamed that I did not wake up in time and Ralph left me there at Mama's and never returned. I jerked awake and looked at the clock. It was time to get up and I felt as though I had not slept at all. My stomach felt sick but there was a cool breeze coming in from the window so I got up and sat looking out into the night. I knew that the truth of my relationship with Ralph would be coming to a head very soon. I was excited and scared at the same time. I sighed and looked up. Mama was standing in the door.

"It's a new day, Johnnie Belle." She smiled at me and left to get ready for work. I pulled on my dress and combed my hair. Then I stood and looked at myself in the faded mirror. I looked like me, but I didn't feel like me. Mama came back.

"Ready?" she asked.

I nodded slowly. I knew I was ready to end the turmoil that had been brewing a storm inside my stomach and chest. I knew I was ready to know the truth about Ralph's feelings for me no matter what they were. I knew I was ready to face the day no matter what it brought. I'd decided that confronting the entire situation was the only way to go on. I needed to know what he wanted and what he felt. He needed to know the same about me. This was foreign territory and I was not sure of myself at all. Was this how Cindy and Cody started, I wondered as I prepared to meet Ralph to head back to Missouri? She did not know that loving a person could be so complicated, so exciting and scary at the same time. She wondered what else there was to learn in her life. Amazed that her life had taken so many turns in the past few months, she wondered about her insecurities and had little confidence in herself.

Chapter 15

Ralph woke up long before the sun. He was eager to get the apples back to Northwest Missouri and he was dreading the heat of the day. Today, though, even more than this job, Johnnie Belle occupied his mind. Since talking it over with Davey and Ruth, Ralph knew that he had their support if he decided to ask Johnnie Belle to marry him. They had their concerns about her being so near Nadine's age, and they were not happy about her being in the house and how it looked. What convinced them was the fact that he seemed to really care about Johnnie Belle and the whole family appeared to be getting along just fine with her. All except for Lynn, but then, he was a handful for anyone. Of course, up to this point, he and Johnnie Belle had managed to ignore the whole issue that loomed between them. He just hoped that he wasn't being a fool.

It was time for him to get his feelings out in the open, at least open between himself and Johnnie. He had to face up to the way she had stirred him inside. He was pretty sure that Johnnie Belle felt the same and Ralph wanted to give her the opportunity to find out if she was really ready to leave her Mother for a life with him in Missouri. He knew that it would be a big step for both of them.

Getting into his truck, he grabbed an apple and ate it. The truck backfired and lurched out onto the road toward Star City. It wasn't a long drive but a hint of light was in the eastern sky as he entered the small town Johnnie Belle called home.

Making an effort to go slow enough as to not stir up the dust, he worked his way across town. Making a sharp right turn he looked down the street towards her house. Her house, like most on this street, was a small shack of a place

211

and needed work. It was a sure sign of the times, Ralph thought.

He could see her sitting in the yard. Her mother was there with her. He watched Johnnie Belle get up from an old chair as he rolled onto the lawn that edged the road and shut off the engine. She was carrying her tote sack and he saw her hug her mother and walk toward the truck. His heart raced for a moment as it confirmed that she was indeed coming back with him and, he hoped, to be a part of his life.

They had a hard day's travel ahead of them so Ralph was grateful that Johnnie Belle was up and ready. As she opened the door and threw her things in, Ralph got out and went over to meet her mother. He owed her that.

"Hello ma'am." Ralph tipped his hat. "I'm Ralph Showalter."

"Hello." She drawled meekly. She was shorter than Johnnie Belle but had the same color eyes and soft voice.

"I want you to know," he looked off towards the house and saw Harold coming out onto the porch, "Ma'am, I want you to know that I will be good to your girl." He said this more as a parent would to another parent, knowing that it was not easy to let a child go, especially so far, and with a man she hardly knew.

"Thank you, Mr. Showalter." Johnnie Belle's mother drawled softly. "You take good care of her. I'm trusting you to do right by her." She smiled at him but had sadness in her eyes. She was only a few years older than him but the lines in her face were deep with the struggles of her life. Harold ran out to the truck where Johnnie Belle was standing and waiting. Ralph glanced at them.

"I will ma'am." Ralph tipped his hat again and walked back to the truck. He knew what her words meant. She meant that he'd better not hurt her in any way. He wondered if Johnnie Belle had talked to her mother about the sparks that had been flying back and forth between them.

"Good morning, Harold." Ralph shook his hand.

"Good morning, Mister Showalter." His hair stuck up and he still had the grit of sleep in his eyes. He yawned.

"Let's go, Johnnie Belle, if you're ready. We've got a hard trip ahead."

Johnnie Belle hugged Harold and jumped in. She waved at her mother and Harold as Ralph turned the engine and rolled slowly down the street.

"Good-bye!" She yelled at them as they stood in the front of the house staring after them.

The morning did not seem to be in a hurry to arrive and the coolness of the night filled the space between them as Ralph picked up speed and headed out of town.

Ralph felt nervous because he was not good at expressing his emotions.

"I see you decided to come back with me."

Johnnie Belle looked at him to see if she could read his face and know what he was thinking. She did know that he usually spoke what was on his mind and if he didn't want her to return he surely would have made that clear. These feelings between them were the best thing about their whole relationship and the worst. They were exciting new feelings for her but they made her crazy all the same.

"Yes," she said simply and felt as nervous as the first time she met him. She thought he sounded funny. It was either because he wished she had made the other choice and stayed with Mama, or because he was glad she was returning with him and his feelings were similar to hers. Her mind clouded with doubt, but she had to know.

"Aren't you glad?" Johnnie Belle asked him. She turned around in the truck to face him as he drove. "I mean, didn't you want me to come back?" Johnnie Belle considered the fact that she could be all wrong about him. All of a sudden she was so unsure of herself. What if she had done the wrong thing? She couldn't go back with him if he did not feel the same things she was feeling. She felt angry, though not knowing if she was angry with herself or Ralph.

Ralph looked at her, saw the anger in her eyes and gave an exasperated sigh. He pulled the truck off the road, shut off the engine and looked at her. He knew that they could not wait any longer. He heard the edginess in her voice and figured she was about to erupt in anger at him. He took a breath and faced her there in the dark, framed by a hint of light and the promise of a new day.

Ralph took Johnnie's hand and held it. Then looking down at the floor he tried to form the right words he wanted to say to her.

Ralph was not sure where to begin. "Johnnie Belle, listen to me." He spoke gently and looked once more into her face.

Johnnie looked back. What was it he was trying so hard to tell her? If it was good, it could not be so hard. So, it was not good. All of a sudden Johnnie Belle felt she must have been wrong. Already tense with emotion, she panicked and knew only one way to make this easy for both of them.

"It's alright. I understand." She pulled away from Ralph and yanked at the handle on the door. "I'll get out here and walk back to Star City. You should have just told me earlier, Ralph." Her heart ached. Her face hurt from the tears that threatened. Johnnie shoved the heavy door outwards.

"Johnnie," Ralph sounded like he did when the girls irritated him.

She turned to look at him once more. "I'm sorry." She tried to say. "I'm sorry to put you in this spot. I didn't intend to fall in love with you. I can't go back with you this way."

But he reached across the seat and pulled her towards him, kissing her lightly then holding her close.

A stunned look spread across her face and the tears fell from her eyes.

"Don't cry, Johnnie Belle. I love you."

Though those were the very words she wanted to hear, in fact, expected to hear, she was openly shocked.

"You mean you really do want me to go back home with you?"

"Yes, I do, Johnnie Belle." Ralph reached over and pulled the door shut. "I want you to come home with me today, now, and I don't want you to ever go away."

"But what about your family?" She moved back away from his arms so that she could look directly into his eyes. "I mean Aunt Emma and Aunt Ruth don't really like me."

"I had a talk with Davey and Ruth and they said they would support us." Ralph couldn't take his eyes from Johnnie's. "Aunt Ruth will talk to Emma and it will be alright. Anyway, I never have done what they want me to do, why should I start now?" Ralph laughed.

I laughed. It felt good and the tension seemed to fall away.

"I thought that since that day Uncle Davey and Aunt Ruth had come over that you were different."

"Well, I was in a way. I made a decision that day and it scared me some."

"Are you still scared?" She asked him.

"Yes." He admitted.

"Me too," Johnnie Belle smiled. "But happy."

Ralph started up the truck and pulled out heading north

up the road. He relaxed his lean frame and put his arm around Johnnie Belle pulling her over closer to him.

The apples bumped back and forth against the sides of the truck, the wind blew wisps of Johnnie's hair around her face, and the sun rose.

Ralph flew over the roads anxious to get on with the journey they had started.

"You know Johnnie, these feeling I have for you took me by surprise." Not being a man who let his guard down often, and also one who likes to hold the reins tightly, Ralph shook his head at himself.

They rode in silence once again but this time with a single purpose. Getting home and moving on.

Johnnie Belle closed her eyes and cuddled into the curve of Ralph's arm. She was tired. Closing her eyes she thought about the change in herself over the past few months. She remembered leaving Star City that first time. She about jumped out of a truck then too. She thought about Cindy and Cody and Jack and that man named Dirk. It had been a long trip indeed to where she was now.

As they rode along toward home, Johnnie Belle worried about Ralph's family, the ladies at church, the children, and how she would cope with all of the tension. As if he was thinking the same things, Ralph tightened his grip around her shoulders.

"Let's make home-made ice cream tomorrow after church if there's any ice left when we get home." Ralph's mind was already back home with Johnnie Belle a part of his life.

"I'd like that." Johnnie Belle breathed deeply, thinking about the coolness of the ice cream, a place where she belonged, and this man who loved her. She'd been living around the edges of life, content, but missing out on the main event. She now dived head on into the center of the rest of her life with Ralph and his family. Things would never be the same, but she didn't want that anymore. They both had just taken the next step. She knew that together they could rise above the dust and face the challenges of the future as one.